Praise for
Sigrún Pálsdóttir

"Absolutely brilliant from beginning to end."
—Halla Oddný Magnúsdóttir, National TV

"An amazing story. . . . A very memorable reading
experience, and in spite of a serious undertone
there's a very finely tuned quiet humor."
—Júlía M. Alexandersdóttir, *Morgunbladid*

"A complex and arresting novel where a super precise
style and an ingenious construction come together."
—Nomination Committee for the Women's Literature Prize

"Like a cubist work of art."
—Jóhanna María Einarsdóttir, *DV*

RY.

A

MESS.

Sigrún
Pálsdóttir

Translated from the Icelandic
by Lytton Smith

OPEN LETTER
LITERARY TRANSLATIONS FROM THE UNIVERSITY OF ROCHESTER

First edition, 2019
All rights reserved

Library of Congress Cataloging-in-Publication Data: Available.
ISBN-13: 978-1-940953-98-4 / ISBN-10:1-940953-98-7

*This project and its translation are both supported in part by
awards from the National Endowment for the Arts*

*This project is supported in part by the New York State Council on the Arts
with the support of Governor Andrew M. Cuomo and the New York State Legislature*

Printed on acid-free paper in the United States of America.

Text set in Garamond, a group of old-style serif typefaces
named after the punch-cutter Claude Garamont.

Design by N. J. Furl

Open Letter is the University of Rochester's nonprofit, literary translation press:
Dewey Hall 1-219, Box 278968, Rochester, NY 14627

www.openletterbooks.org

S. B., Diary for 1642/1643.
Bod. MS. 3971
(Pick) 8vo

This day, after I was redie, I did eate my breakfast.

Day 201. And with these words, I had written this same sentence out two hundred and one times. And, following on from it, the paragraph comprising each journal entry. The task had already taken me about six months: despite the incessant repetition, the linguistic nuances in this cramped ancient manuscript were significant enough to cause me considerable labors. And still the result was always the same: nothing of note. Nothing but rigid, rather uninspiring testimony to a humble existence, an existence to which it was practically impossible to accord any greater meaning, even though it was 365 years old. But I was determined to finish, to keep following the thread. To keep scrutinizing nothing. And so I did until it hit me. Much longer than all the other entries, a piece that opened with one, and only one, heading:

The day 203

This was around noon, but by the time I had made my way through both pages, it was closing time at the library. I looked at my transcription. It took me a little while to fully realize what I'd discovered:

> *This day, after I was redie, I did eate my breakfast. Went down finding my father gone to London. After I finished the picture of Lady Cowley in little I Painted over ye 3d Time a side face of Mrs Meriton. Lady Bucks picture done over with white poppy oil as thin done over as I could.*
>
> *That done Mr. Jones, who stayes at My Lords house, came hither to the Paynting roome for his final sitting of his picture done upon 3 qtr Sacking. Mr Jones sat with admirable and unvariable patience. He is a very excellent young man & by whose conversacon I learn to observe the very glancing of his eyes. Every lowly grace of his face. He sat for 4 hourse tell I had pfectly finisht ye face to my owne satisfaction. He thought his picture mighty like him and colored exceedingly rarely but the colouring of the face to be a little forced.*
>
> *Mr Jones being out of doors I did some thing about the house tell my father was back from his journey with a pacell of Pink made by Mr Petty and another of blew black and primed paper for study. After we supped on pease porridge and bread I went to Ye Chamber. After reading of the Humanitie I was busie fouldinge some linan and airinge clothes tell all most night. So to bed wher many sundrie distractions withdrew my mind so I was weak and had paine in my head.*

The custodian at the manuscript library, a young, athletic man, rested his hand lightly and just for a moment on my shoulder. Then he tapped the index finger of the same hand against his delicate watch. I closed the book at once, returned it to its box and gave it to him. I gathered my things together, rose from the table, walked out of the room, slowly passing along the long hallway, all the way trying to hold back the smile that played behind my lips. There was no doubt the creator of that famous portrait of Viscount Tom Jones was my diary writer, S. B. But could it be that S. B. was a woman? *Busie fouldinge some linan and airinge clothes?* A trailblazer? Had I just found a new beginning in the history of Western art? Frenzied jubilation thrilled through my body, words burst within me freighted with tremendous power, inside my head sentences and then pages formed one after the other so that by the time I stepped out of the building into the outside courtyard, my introduction was well underway.

Out on the street, nothing was the same. I wasn't the same. I could sense it in the slightest gesture, the way my arms swung back and forth, my hips moving rhythmically side to side, my hair billowing in the warm spring breeze, and by the time I had turned onto the path that leads to the church and had gone past a young man with a guitar—at which point I entirely surprised myself by letting a ten-pound note float down into his case—my thesis was fast taking shape. It was practically fully formed by the time I left the city center, those beautiful surroundings to which I belonged during the day and which made all my miniscule, dispensable thoughts about life in centuries past worth anything each day. Reflections which had hitherto somewhat lost their meaning when I, at the end of my workday, left the ancient buildings and headed home to the grim, inescapable existence that was my part of the city: Low-rise precast concrete houses. Grouped in long rows. Washed out in a monotone overcoat the color of cream. Seventies residences that seemed about to collapse under the conflicts taking place inside them.

My neighbor slammed her front door behind her and strode rapidly away from the house while the shouting from inside her home fell silent. I do not remember how she responded to my greeting as we passed; I was lost in my reflections, unaware whether I said hello to her, so deep was I in thought over the day's discovery. By now, I had the whole introduction in my head. Time for the preface. I would, of course, express gratitude to Professor Lucy for having entrusted this large project to me, and to Dr. Caplan and his colleagues for their advice and for something I might call inspiration. To Mrs. Mary Howard for teaching me to read the old hand. And perhaps it would be right to mention all the help I'd received from people at the museum. The young custodian in the manuscript library? Presumably he would be helping me more in the foreseeable future. Was it going to be five years of work? For a moment, it even dawned on me to thank the professors at the Royal College of Art for having ruthlessly rejected me, an event that had indirectly pushed me toward this international discipline, art history, in which I was now bound to play a major role. No, the idea was just a bit of fun; better to nourish the joy now stirring inside me after the difficulties and disappointments of the past year. But next I would absolutely thank Dad and my friend Sigga. Possibly Bonný and Tína too, for being such a source of amusement and encouragement. And Hans, of course. Maybe for having made the decision to complete his own studies here, which meant I ended up in exactly this place and not somewhere else. No, surely I could find something better to say about Hans. There was time enough for that. But Mom? How to thank her? The answer was obvious, and came to me by the time I inserted my key in the lock on the flame-red front door: the thesis would, of course, be dedicated to my mother!

I closed the door behind me. Hans wasn't home. I stood in the middle of the living room, looked down at the beige carpet, and imagined the letters printed on the white page immediately following the flyleaf: *To my mother*. Then I heard a heavy thud from the other side of the thin partition wall, as though someone had kicked it: "Bugger!" My neighbor, getting ready for the evening. I lay on the couch, laced my fingers behind my neck. I looked at the card panels trying to free themselves from the ceiling above me, and thought that it would perhaps be more beautiful this way: *For my mother*.

Six Hundred Pages Later
In Another City:
Reykjavík

Hallway

"And then what?" I'm the one asking the question. Here in my dressing gown. In a conversation I'm beginning to fear will have no end.

"Well," says my sister-in-law, vacantly, an automated prelude to what follows: "I simply pointed out to them that one way out of the problem was for everybody to sit down and write out all the things that trouble them about their working conditions." There's a short pause as she dangles her keychain ring from her middle finger and conceals it in her palm like castanets; she sets off along the hallway, taking slow steps as her lips let out these words: "For just as the written word can help people express complex feelings, through it we can also recognize and understand the insignificance and frivolity of the problems we face. Or, as they say, everything looks better on paper!"

And now, all at once, I feel her words somehow directed toward me in particular, feel that I must now start writing down whatever nonsense I can—but then I stop thinking about it, because as my sister-in-law's account of the bruised egos in her departmental meeting approaches its peak with a description of the excessive response one of her colleagues made to the idea of these "worry notes," her statement that "everything looks better on paper," I notice a door on the living room wall. It's a door I don't feel I've noticed before. I get up and stand deathly still while I stare at it before me, but my sister-in-law has reached the front door. She is now talking about baggage and boxes, all the metaphors of this hobbyhorse of hers and is more like herself than she was. Because, despite her social standing, despite being part of Icelandic academia, it's unusual for her to use words like *frivolous*. Less so *the written word*, which is so clearly absurd in her case, but there's no time to reflect on that now as I make my way out of the living room in her wake, heading toward the entrance, pondering this door in my head while waiting for her to show herself out.

My sister-in-law has grasped the knob and is about to open the door, but hesitates an eternal moment as she realizes that she has forgotten to ask me how I'm doing. Her rhetorical question comes in the form of a suggestion that maybe I should use my sick leave, "I mean, this period of time," to read her latest blogpost: "The Great Importance of the Present Moment." She roughly explains the gist to me, guides the conversation to another topic, and reminds me to talk to "that Diana." Finally wraps things up: "Alright, hon, talking cures." She turns the knob without opening the door while she tugs, unsuccessfully, her tiny denim jacket's bodice over her ample bosom and says: "The final spurt can be almost everlasting, I remember when I finished my own thesis and . . ."—and with this the front door opens. And with it the heavens open! Black clouds stand out against light pillows that stand out against the sunshine and the calm skies, and I stare into the open endlessness, into the beauty I once dreamed about depicting, and I cannot help but once again rehearse the event that put an end to all those intentions. But there is nothing to be done, and I start pondering something unrelated, not coming to my senses until the scattering of birds from a huge oak tree in the park on the other side of the street, swooping up into flight; I study my sister-in-law's carefully ruffled chestnut hair as she takes heavy but carefree steps away from my house. Ready to wrestle with some new scientific mystery of human interaction and behavior. All the pregnant moments in time the confused people of this world forget to enjoy. The academic delegate for the growing business of mindfulness and life-coaching whose own existence is predicated on the message that each person's problem is hidden from themselves.

I close the door and push my face up against it. The great importance of the moment. I draw deep breaths and then walk, overly quiet, practically backward, into the living room. It's no more than three or four steps. How can I have missed seeing this door in the six whole days I've been living here? Was it here yesterday? I don't dare answer that question right away; I sit on the couch and retrieve the crumbled rectangle of paper, the business card my sister-in-law handed me, from my clenched palm; I caress it and try to smooth it flat.

Díana D. Lárusdóttir

Life Coach

Member of The International Coach Federation (ICF)

*Fear is that little darkroom
where misconceptions are developed.*

Right! I feel myself dissolving as I sit here trying to see myself through my sister-in-law's eyes and in the company of the person named on the card. Who was she to say goodbye the way she had? Had she figured out my situation? As soon as I pose these questions, it occurs to me that her loquacity is a telltale sign she suspects I'm facing something more than a severe headache. That I have some kind of theoretical dilemma: "The final spurt can be almost everlasting." Intuition, or drivel?

For now, I lean toward the latter; I stand up and stick the card in my dressing gown pocket. I walk toward the door. It's slightly shorter than the rest of the doors in the apartment. I run my fingers over the door's plain surface, grab the handle and start to push it down. Then I break off, relaxing my grip; I bend down and gently put my face up against the door, one eye to the keyhole. At first, there's nothing but darkness, so black it's like there's nothing inside, as though the wall is right up against the door. Eventually, the darkness dilutes and I think I discern a faint light a distance back. I straighten up and regard the door. I knock on the wall around the doorframe. Then I grab the handle quickly and go to open it. The door, of course, doesn't budge. I start to shove and push the door, to pull at it, suddenly stopping when I sense someone standing behind me.

My husband, Hans. In front of me, now. Me here with the door at my back. Where did he come from so suddenly, here in the living room with two shopping bags, his face at once questioning and smiling? "What?" I say. He replies, "What what?" Kisses me and smirks. Then he takes the bags into the kitchen. I trail behind him.

Why hasn't anyone mentioned this door since we moved in? Perhaps for the same reason as the truth about my many years of research refuses to come to the surface: I cannot, of course, bring myself to think about it, no, not so much as put it into words inside my own head. And all around me there's a wonderful silence, a momentary understanding that there's been a little dent to my health, nothing more, that has caused my studies to have been suspended for the foreseeable future.

I cut some vegetables, wondering how to find words for the topic. How to phrase this question: "What's that door in the living room, Hans?" "There's a door in the living room?" "Hans, did you notice that door?" "You know, I never noticed that door until today." Perhaps it's more than just a matter of phrasing, I think, and take the hot dish out of the oven; as we sit down at the table, I realize that time is running away from me. Or, rather, that it isn't working in my favor: after having set the table, my opportunity to articulate my question has gone. Or am I deliberately second-guessing my words? Am I creating suspense and expectation out of the unsaid, seeking something to rack my brain over amid my intolerable existence? Might I have taken it upon myself to imagine a door, given the dead-end my life has run into? Unless, perhaps, this is the door of that "little darkroom" that houses all the false ideas only the Diana D.s of this world can correct.

I look down at my plate. Nothing is about to happen here. How could my life undergo so much change in so short a time and yet return to the same conformity this absurd picture of the two of us here at the table suggests? I look at Hans chewing his food but hear nothing. So comfortable in his own skin, tender in some remote way, but when I tell him about his sister's visit and everything she had to say, he looks at me in a way that says, despite everything, we're in this together. Because Hans perceives the gap between me and the others, and nothing ties two people together more tightly than that kind of understanding. Even if that person can seem occasionally distant, like Hans, so lost in his world that if you don't reach out, grasp hold of him, he floats away, as he's doing now, as I'm letting him do. I'm still trying to figure out what his reaction would be if I reached out for him and laid my cards on the table. Cards on the table. I suspect that his reaction would be sensible. And prudence is no use to me now. My problem calls for a radical solution.

His seat is turned so that whoever sits there only need glance into the living room to be confronted by the door. And Hans does that as he pauses amid some funny story from his laboratory, trying to recall the name of the employee in question. I look at his eyes looking toward the door, but that's no use in working out if he sees it; his gaze is so remote, his search focused on the lost name. Suddenly he looks away from the door and straight into my eyes: "Valmundur!" The employee's name. But by this time, I've already lost the thread.

We stand up from the table and Hans concludes his story inside the kitchen, after which he strolls off and I'm left standing alone at the sink; it strikes me that the door is on the outer wall. And there is no window on that wall. I go into the living room and look out of the front window of the building, the window closest and perpendicular to the windowless side, and try to see if the distance from the corner of the room is the same inside and outside. But there's no way to make sure from here, my face pressed against the glass. I'd better go out and check. How hollow was the sound when I knocked on the wall around the door? And where is Hans? He's gotten into bed, his face behind a book; facing him, along a direct line of sight through the bedroom doors and hallway, is the door.

Hardly; half the door. From his side of the bed. I see so for myself when I come to bed and find an excuse to lean in his direction, peeking up from my book about a man who paints pictures on pencil boxes and thinks about death. I turn back to the book and continue to travel the pages without knowing where the story's heading, my thoughts erasing the meaning of the words as soon as I've read them. My inner turmoil constantly whirrs away, destroying all the story's innumerable little details that should click together to form the complete meaning of this finely-wrought, dust-jacketed book's message, a message I will not locate any time soon, for my eyes start to close and the book is on top of my face. But just before that happens, I get this brilliant idea.

Then she smiles slyly, almost warmly,
as she fetches a little book and
holds it out toward me

As soon as Hans closes the door behind him, I get up and rush to
the basement. Down the steps, stroking the light-green stone wall,
the paint that hides a mural I have murky memories of from having come to this house once as a child. Inside the storage space, I
reach past a black plastic bag full of empty glass bottles to pick up
what lies rolled up on the bottom shelf opposite the door. I take
the fabric roll in my arms and hold it out in front of me.

When I get back upstairs, I unroll the material on the living room floor, smoothing it out: Atropos, Lachesis, and Clotho
have spun their thread and cut it, standing with their toes planted
on their prey. Death overcomes a chaste maiden. Something of
that sort. A reproduction of a much larger tapestry, something we
bought right before moving back to Iceland. I lift the hanging up
off the floor and remember why it's been rolled up in storage since
we moved in a week ago: I haven't yet found a way to hang it. But
now there's only one solution; I have the hammer in one hand
and five long nails in the other. I push the chest, which stands in
the middle of the living room like a table, across the floor to the

wall and climb up on it. I drive the nails into the wall above the door frame, clamber down from the chest, drag the fabric behind me and stretch the upper margin across the nails. The hanging does not quite cover the door all the way to the floor, but I just stack books and other stuff carelessly in front of it.

I sit on the couch and regard the setup. I've hidden what can't be seen, fearing it's only visible to me. But I've also done this to nurture an old dream, wanting my living space to be more than what can be seen. Hazy suspicion about doors and mysterious nooks gets proved; beside the corner is a small staircase right up against the wall. Just a few steps, leading up to the door, the door that opens into a dim room, the room that opens out to a beautiful garden. And from there I can look out onto green fields. Until I recover my senses and face my disappointment; hazy suspicion about doors and mysterious nooks gets disproved.

I'm bored. I look at them, *The Three Fates, the Moirai*. Atropos's green-blue dress and the golden twig-belt, the flowers creamy and crimson against the night-blue background. An ancient agricultural scene that now conceals what's probably nothing more than the door to a locked storage compartment containing flotsam from the estate to which our apartment belongs. I push the books on the floor gently away from the door, sneak my hand behind the tapestry, and tug the handle. I hold it down, but instead of pulling it toward me like yesterday, I jiggle it a bit to the side and wrest it in circles to try to better release the latch from its hole in the frame. A click. The door budges and starts to pull the fabric away from the wall, so I push it closed again. I open it a slender crack, stick my head under the tapestry and peer into the darkness. The air is thick but smells of some kind of cleaning fluid. Of old cleanliness. Taking shape before me I see a small windowless room. Empty, except for the wall opposite the door, where there hangs a golden frame. And, from the ceiling on the right, something white dangles, some material, but as I move to open the door further and stretch my hand inside to see what that is, I hear a knock behind me. Someone is hammering on the front door. Two heavy determined blows. I close the door, smooth down the tapestry, and traipse along into the hallway.

Two older women are standing on the steps outside the house. They are dressed in trench coats. Poplin. One of the two, almost a head taller than her companion, wishes me good day and gets right to the matter, a question about whether I ever think about the amount of soap I use for cleaning and other hygienic purposes here at home. And without giving me a chance to answer, she hands me a folio sheet folded in four. On the front, there's a pencil drawing of a man with shoulder-length hair and open arms. Jesus. Christ. The woman holds the paper in her outstretched hand, but under the sleeve of her coat I see her shirt. Polyester. Paisley. I look away, down at the floor, where the woman has stuck her foot over the threshold. A brown leather shoe, laced over swollen insteps. Custom-made? Orthopedic? I look up as I move to close the door. The woman jerks her foot out; as they are bidding me farewell, they turn out not to be as old as I thought they were at first. I take the little booklet into the kitchen and throw it into the bucket under the sink, where the fish Hans took out of the freezer this morning are lying in a sieve. Ready for the soup I'd intended to spend my day preparing. I place both hands on my head. An impending ache.

From inside the kitchen I analyze every gesture. Mom takes off her silk-soft cashmere coat and hands it to Dad, who hangs it in the closet while Hans helps my Aunt Gréta out of her garment. It's not a coat but a thin, crumpled windbreaker. A kind of purple. Then Hans comes into the kitchen to fetch drinks as I go into the living room and sit on the sofa next to my father. Gréta sits opposite us in a chair, but the inspector doesn't sit right away. Mom never sits right away. She stands and scrutinizes the surroundings and watches. Now she can seize her moment, here in this apartment rented off the estate of her parents' childhood friend: "Is this what you bought in London?" She crosses to the wall hanging and scowls when she sees the nails poking out from the top. She slides her gold-plated glasses down to the rounded tip of her nose, takes the edge of the tapestry and pulls it taut to more closely examine the image; her plump, smooth face is framed by her silver-gray bob. My mother is blunt, yet somehow still frail, unlike Gréta, who is sitting behind her sister, listening to her give a short disquisition on Flemish medieval weaving and Petrarchan poetry. Gréta is delicately built yet sturdy, with short hair; slender, cheap gold threads dangle from her ears. Her shirt fabric has indistinct pencil-strokes, but on her shoulders there is some modest padding and the garment is buttoned up to the neck; it's a bit difficult to say whether my mother's sister looks more feminine or masculine. She is a systems analyst, introverted and sometimes a bit rough, but still with some warmth in her manner, just like how Mom's gentle, calculated appearance can sometimes seem distant and cold, as it does now, once she's finished her speech and thoughtfully inspects the ceiling, still holding the edge of the tapestry between her index finger and thumb so that, from where Dad sits beside me on the couch, the door is exposed. I stand up, walk over to her, and flatten the tapestry so that she loses her grip and the door disappears. "Dinner is served!" My words emerge from Hans's mouth as he appears at that exact moment from the dining room.

As I'm ladling soup into Gréta's bowl, I call to mind the white material I thought I saw hanging from the ceiling in the room behind the door. I suppose there must have been a sheet over some stuff stored there, or so I think as I hand Gréta her bowl. She vigorously nods thanks, because Mom has started to talk so slowly and so quietly that the least sound would cause her listeners to lose the thread of her story, about a young, up-and-coming Icelandic artist. She's mastered this style little by little since deciding to finally take her high-school exams and go to college at the age of 50, having abruptly left school as a teenager. That historical fact is the foundation of the complex relationship between her and Gréta, who was buried in books but stumbled terribly in her personal life—she's thrice-divorced—whereas Mom thrived triumphantly with her lackey by her side, a doctor and gentle soul who seemingly has an unstoppable need to push her forward as a great intellect. Beyond logic, beyond what would be considered normal for a loving marriage. After Mom completed her university degree, achieving very good results, as a matter of fact, her strength has primarily been in her good taste for knowledge; she is a connoisseur of what one ought to know at any given moment, and liable to disseminate that knowledge to those who don't care for it: "There is in her work a jarring clash between tradition and revolution, I think she's working with our history in ways no Icelandic artist has ever done."

Although I've never heard my mother talk about the person under discussion, this conversation has happened before. In form. That is, if I accord the proper significance to the expressions on Greta's lips and Dad's head movements as Mom begins to describe the work, giant portraits of Icelandic national leaders from the past two centuries. Four times two meters in area, composed of several hundreds of mirror fragments which, by dint of the discriminating color of each piece of glass and its position in the larger image, reveal two different faces, male and female, depending on from where the work is viewed. Another part of the work is the viewer's multifaceted reflection in the image, the figurative sculpture standing before it.

Suddenly Mom falls silent, looking toward me; for a moment I think she might be going to use this anecdote to put my own study on the agenda here at the dinner table, thereby breaking the silent agreement that has reigned regarding my studies since Hans and I decided to return home. But luckily this does not transpire because Gréta takes the reins, asking her sister about the work's specific message. "Is it a question about whether the vantage you look from matters?" she asks, hovering over her soup bowl, tilting it and scraping her spoon along the bottom. But it's Dad who is first to answer; he leans back in his chair, turns to Mom with a smile on his lips, and tells us that magic resides in art just as in science. Then he lifts his glass and thanks us for dinner without reflecting on the meaning of his words. Indeed, there's no meaning. Only a wretched, involuntary attempt to achieve peace where there is neither force nor really any particular warfare, an attempt to flatten reality, and perhaps to defend Mom. But Dad has no need to defend Mom; she can answer for herself, and does so now with a deep silence as Gréta and I talk about the alleged adultery of a minor celebrity, then move onto a television series Mom seems not to know. In fact, Mom does not say much for the rest of the evening, not until we've moved on to coffee and Gréta is telling me about a novel she's just finished reading that has sold over three million copies. Then Mom speaks, quietly from behind pursed lips, reciting words that are written on her countenance, a countenance no one can read but me:

"My poor Gréta, captivated by such tastelessness. A fiction taking its inspiration from the imagistic expositions of the American entertainment industry, rather than coming into being as a continuation of literary tradition, stemming from the written word." And then she goes on about all the pointless efforts the authors of such books exert to tie things together, filling in all the holes, tying everything into a neat bow, without the slightest hint of subtext. To construct all these subplots with their carefully orchestrated roles in the greater elaboration of the denouement that turns the whole story upside down, and unsettles the reader entirely, butting up against his sense of justice and humanity. But the endings, like the turning points in the narrative, are not as unpredictable as they first appear because they always follow a certain formula: the pre-scripted unpredictability. Mom leans back. She seems troubled as she breathes out a final bubble: "And in the world of commercial fiction, these formulae become markers of quality, gaining traction in the useless agreement booklovers have made to revive the author's social responsibility, the idea that an author's work should have an agenda, should speak directly to his contemporaries and, more than anything else, be immediately in their service. But then who is going to take care of aesthetics, that's what I ask," Mom asks.

And that's right! That, at the very end, I mean, the sixpence in the pudding, is the unexpected ending of that bestseller, a conclusion that left Gréta stymied, mouth shut tight. I should read the book, she insists, promising to lend me her copy as she kisses me goodbye. Before my absent-minded mother takes me aside and tells me in no uncertain terms that I need to take better care of myself and go out for walks. Go for walks? Sounds like a smart solution to my problem, I think, and nod my head hopelessly at my mother. The way she evades my glance suggests she knows I'm in a pinch from which no turn about the streets, no plot twist, can save me.

Once the three guests have left the apartment and are out on the sidewalk, Mom suddenly raises both hands in the air and turns around. She walks back up the stone steps and roots around in her big handbag, the one with the little gold-plated clasp. Then she smiles slyly, almost warmly, as she fetches a little book and holds it out toward me. She doesn't allow me the opportunity to thank her, hastening off in the direction of the glistening, silver-gray Jeep that my Dad has started up, the tired Gréta in the backseat. I watch the car slip along the street as I stroke the bright pink, soft leather binding. I tug at the delicate golden thread that closes it. A notebook. A luxury item from her last trip to Italy, bestowed upon her only child.

*I set the manuscript down on the table
and thought to myself it was probably the
last time I'd handle the old tome*

In a dream, my cheek is being beaten with a little hammer. Just lightly and high up on the cheekbone, but the noise of the blow is so loud my head shakes and reverberates. I open my eyes and hide under the blanket. Someone outside the house is using a pneumatic drill. I slide my hand gently out toward the bedside table and grab my pillbox. As I do, light sidles its way inside my cave, and I realize nothing in here can protect me from the merciless midday sun because my mom could not tolerate the old, overly ornate curtains that were up and so she tore them down. Before any replacements had been bought, naturally. I potter into the living room hugging the blanket around me. And there it appears before me, the entrance into perfect darkness.

I put the blanket on the couch and walk toward the door. It opens easily and I angle myself under the wall hanging and go in. I close it behind me and sit down in the corner beside the door. On the hard, cold floor, wearing my thin nightdress, my knees up to my chest. But the darkness in here feels good, so strangely quiet compared to the hullabaloo outside the house. I lean my head up against the wall and keep my eyes closed as I wait for the pain to intensify.

Occasionally, I open my eyes. Through the keyhole creeps a tiny amount of faint light, which grows brighter once I grow accustomed to the darkness. And now I can see the gold frame's outline on the wall opposite the door. I put my arms on my knees and tilt my head down only to immediately look back up. Something is moving in the corner of the room. I have to squint through the darkness and finally I shift myself and there, four feet in front me, is something I cannot distinguish or comprehend. It seems to come and go, then appears long enough for me to make it out: a very tiny woman, naked and entirely peculiar in her proportions, facing the wall. In her sitting position, she can hardly be more than ten centimeters tall. She seems to be sketching on a large card she has in her over-sized hand. It isn't giant, but flat, like a broad leaf. The woman sits with her side to me but I can still somehow see both her eyes. Her nose is big and crooked, but there's no chin. Her thin hair has been swept into a ponytail at the nape of her neck. Her feet are like her hand but her breasts are neat and somehow stiff in appearance, in no way consistent with the surreal, freeform shape of her body. On the floor in front of her, a tiny mirror leans against the wall, so she is probably drawing herself. I reach my hand toward her, my index finger extended, but just then I hear my name being called. And simultaneously the woman disappears. I get up and carefully take hold of the handle. I crack the door and slip out from under the tapestry. And when I close it carefully behind me, I hear Hans slamming the bathroom door.

I did not notice when he came out of the bathroom, only vaguely became aware of him standing behind me, how he put his hands around my sore head and kissed my crown. I'm sitting balled up on the sea-green plush chair under the window, left behind for us tenants by the house's owners. With my back to the room, hands over my eyes, thinking of flower faeries and dwarves. Of the miniscule creatures who would glide across my bed as a little girl right before I dragged myself to my parents' bed to share my headache. About the little officer who guarded the toothbrush in the bathroom, the miniature bullfighter who puffed himself up at whatever was on my plate, as though he wanted to rejoice that I had managed to wash down the last of the liver sausage with my milk. I would look up to observe my parents' reactions, which were non-existent; when I looked back down at my plate the Spaniard had disappeared. Nothing to see except the many suet pellets I had industriously pulled from my sausage and carefully arranged on the rim of my plate. But the more I thought about these little people, they all felt like they must have been some dream memory that had made it into real life.

Now I knew that wasn't so. Neither were the overgrown creatures who sometimes stood at the foot of my bed when I was a child staying over at someone else's house. Flickering outlines of blurred human figures seen in my half-awake state, rooms constantly moving. Walls shifting to and fro. Just like had happened a month ago:

Professor Lucy had given the green light and I was finishing up the dissertation. Tying up loose ends. Everything was clicking together and spring was in the air. I set the manuscript down on the table and thought to myself it was probably the last time I'd handle the old tome. A sense of loss and a relief. All I had left now

was a single word in a single sentence in a lone entry. I was unsure
if I had transcribed it right. It was on day 221. Near the end of
the journal. I found the page immediately and swiftly scanned the
text. But something wasn't right, I couldn't find the sentence. In
fact, there was nothing I recognized in the text, nothing I understood at a glance. I soon realized that this was not the same text I
had transcribed. It was one page earlier. In other words, there were
two entries with the same number. And it seemed to be the case
that I had only transcribed one of them. The earlier one. I did not
know how I had scrolled past the second entry even though it was
listed as the same day and for a moment I wondered if I should
even bother to pore through the text; one entry was hardly likely
to change much. But I did not have to read far to see what it
was, just glance at a few words. That caused me to read the entry
carefully. And to read it again and again in the hope that these
few sentences would change their meaning, that they might be
understood in any other way than the one presenting itself to me.

I looked around. Where was I? I looked back at the book,
watching the letters fall down the pages, changing to numerals,
numbers to hours, days and years. Amounts. Pounds. How many
of them were there? Sixty thousand? And where had I taken them
from again? I set my trembling hands on the open book, looked
at the manuscript custodian, the older one, in conversation with
my first-year teacher, Professor Barrington, over at the front desk.
There were a few other people around. Impeccable, respected
scholars who narrowed their eyes at me then turned away and
smiled contentedly to themselves as they continued with what
they were doing. Who had decided to let me in here? Who had
thought it a good idea to let my hands touch this ancient manuscript? I closed the book and stood up from the table without

putting it back in the box. Then I set off down the long hallway with my eyes on the decorative glass at its end. But it did not matter how long I walked, I could not seem to get nearer to the end, to the door out of the hall. The walls seemed to follow me, they moved toward me and away, floating with their beautifully bound books ten meters up into the rafters.

I don't remember having left the building, but I remember being outside a grocery store near my home. Inside the adjacent alley. What was I doing there? Had I thrown up behind the trash can? I have no memory of how I got home, but once I got there I didn't have any medication, not that it really mattered as I don't remember having felt much pain. Except I did feel pain. Pain so deep that when Hans told me he had been offered a position back home, I decided to follow him. I'd gotten sick. I needed to rest before I could finish.

I get up from the sea-green plush and go into the kitchen, past the hallway mirror, a woman in a thin nightgown with uncombed mouse-gray hair down to her shoulders. I take some cookbooks from a drawer. Appetizers. Grilled sandwiches with asparagus and goat cheese, baguettes with artichoke and goat cheese, tomato pie with goat cheese, baked bread with asparagus salad, asparagus salad with artichoke and goat cheese. I put my shaking hand to my mouth. Hans is on the phone to a friend. Talking about tomorrow night. He's going out while I host my old girlfriends. All seven of them.

So it's not exactly a real conversation

At the round table. Bonný, Ester, Sigga A., Sigga D., Tína, Bjarnfríður Una, and Guðbjörg. Bonný the anthropologist; Ester the
nurse, the coach's wife; Sigga A. the biochemist; Sigga D. the
engineer; Tína the freelance actress, of her own volition, by her
own account; Bjarnfríður Una the political candidate; Guðbjörg,
between jobs; Bonný, graying and now a doctoral candidate. Ester,
chestnut haired and olive-skinned, living in a forest-green town-
house in the suburbs with several sons and a husband unhappy
with his lot; Sigga A., light haired, expert and acclaimed in her
field, married but childless, inscrutable and more distant with the
passing years; Sigga D., my favorite, also light-haired but only
down to her shoulders, the mother of two girls, pictured in her
company's brochure wearing a safety helmet; Tína, full of plans,
opinions, and with the longest hair, light red; Bjarnfríður Una,
her hair cropped uncompromisingly short; Guðbjörg, all of a sudden a realtor boasting ten microscopic images in her newspaper
advertisement, pallid, bad skin; Bonný, heading to some conference on some topic or other; Ester, never heading anywhere; Sigga
A., keeping quiet when the conversation turns to people's health;

Sigga D., helping others along; Tína striving to come to know everything between heaven and earth, roughly; Bjarnfríður Una, wearing Icelandic-crafted jewelry around her neck, passing biting judgment on contemporary society, individual initiative and self-reliance; Guðbjörg, a self-professed nerd, wearing costume jewelry bought at thirty thousand feet, claiming some particular thing is surreal; Bonný, divorced but now a part of a European research network, declaring something is epic; Ester, "yes, yes"; Sigga A., filthy rich, wearing frameless glasses; Sigga D., looking for common ground; Tína, claiming to be an introvert and talking about political theater, the theater's conversation with the nation; Bjarnfríður Una cutting off Tína's words about political theater; Guðbjörg trying to reinforce Tína's words about political theater; Bonný discussing coffee; Ester discussing chocolate; Sigga A. and silence; Sigga D. discussing coffee and chocolate; Tína discussing chocolate and coffee; Bjarnfríður Una discussing red wine; Guðbjörg discussing white wine; Bonný talking about a book that takes place in the Middle Ages; Tína talking about the same book; Bonný connecting; Tína too: "Think about it, all of you, twelve hundred years and nothing's changed!" Bonný talking about the past as a mirror of the nation; Tína about the past as a source of self-esteem; Bonný about mindfulness and being fully present; Ester about mindfulness; Sigga A. heading to the bathroom; Sigga D. talking about mindfulness; Tína about mindfulness; Bjarnfríður Una not entirely sure about mindfulness; Guðbjörg pretty sure; Bonný about herself and something else; Ester about herself and something else; Sigga D. about Ester and the same; Sigga A. returning from the toilet; Tína about herself and one other thing; Bjarnfríður about herself and one more thing; Guðbjörg about herself and a completely different thing; Bonný, wearing a fur collar at some opening party; Ester wearing a fur collar but not at any party; Sigga A. wearing a fur collar at some opening party; Sigga D. wearing a fur collar at some opening party; Tína, not wearing a fur collar but still at some opening party; Bjarnfríður Una wearing a fur collar at some opening party; Guðbjörg wearing a fur collar at some opening party; Bonný, Ester, Sigga A., Sigga D., Tína, Bjarnfríður Una, Guðbjörg. And me. With a fur collar?

Each woman's speech begins with one and the same personal pronoun; the next speaker usually makes no effort to understand the previous speaker's perspective, only picks up the thread to serve her own story. So it's not exactly a real conversation. And thus the merry-go-round continues apace until it stops as one of them, quite by chance, manages to make a profound contribution to the discussion, and sweeps away the ugly deliquescence of so many little things. Most often that's Tína, and she finds it no problem to corral Bjarnfríður, too. As the former asks the meaning of economic growth in one part of the world if famine, violence, and ferocious disturbances claw their way into another part, I stand up and clear the empty dishes off the table. I put the crockery in my sink and let the jet of water drown out the suffocation of these recurrent conflicts, scraping away remnants of goat cheese, tomatoes and asparagus, all the while wondering what shapes people's opinions, whether they're maintained by actual conviction or just stubbornness based on some old belief that perhaps owes itself to chance anyway, to some coincidence or to bad company. And that leads me to ponder other people's relationships. I think about the past, how strange it is, how ancient. Then I grab the third wine bottle of the six people had brought me, and feel heat rise to my face at the thought of the missing seventh bottle and my guess as to who chose to come to this gathering empty-handed. But when I walk back into the dining room, it occurs to me that the dissolving of the vexed relationships at the round table seems somehow integral to the system. That is, the mechanism isn't propelled by these women's disposition to agreement alone, but more because most of them, especially Sigga A., Ester and Guðbjörg, a pointed formation, long ago decided to go through life without forming opinions on all the conflicts flaring up all around the world, without trying to get to the bottom of their source or fathom what they're about. And that is how it happened: from the memories of their school years, those developmental moments, these women spin the fine, tremendously strong thread that has ever since bound them together, ensuring peace and joy and laughter for the remainder of the evening.

And everyone wanted their words to be heard more than once that evening, so much so that I forgot the questions that I thought ought to have been in the air ever since this group of women walked into the dining room.

"Right," he said, smirking
as though he'd half expected me

Lucy. Drawn from the Latin name Lucius and entering into the native English tongue via the Norman invasion of England in 1066. The most audacious of my fellow students, or mainly the men, mocked him from time to time, but they were of course so obviously just trying to conceal the terrified respect they had for him. My respect for Lucy was not mixed with fear. I only feared him. What's more, his behavior toward me made it clear he didn't expect much from me. If you really could call it behavior: I was never completely clear whether he knew who I was during the first year of my studies, although I was formally his student. It was not until the first year was over that he called me in for a meeting.

I left my house early in the morning and as I was midway between my house and the building where he had his office it started to rain; I clutched my coat around me and ran. That didn't do anything to prevent me from arriving at my destination drenched; what's more, it meant that I arrived not only wet but also panting.

Professor Lucy directed me to a seat with a silent, firm gesture. He was on the phone. I sat down, caught my breath, but could hardly relax in the deep leather chair that had glued itself to my sopping coat. In front of me was a low table; on top of it were stacks of books and papers, and Lucy sat on the other side of this, at his desk, his back turned to me, which looked out through an old stained-glass window. From his conversation, one could tell he was unhappy with the person to whom he was speaking. But I could not ascertain why; the conversation took place in Spanish and it ended angrily, something I saw as much as heard because Lucy broke off the conversation by hanging up on the person at the other end of the line. I watched his neck tense above his chairback, how he slid his hands down his face in reaction before he turned his chair around away from his desk at a snail's pace.

We were facing one another. He leaned back, crossing his feet to reveal his red nylon socks and white, hairless tibia. He straightened his pants leg at the thigh to stop his knees bursting through the linen. He looked at me like he was still thinking about the phone call and right away I sensed the distance between us. It was something much bigger than these stacks of books, this little table and the oriental rug underneath it. And there was nothing I could do about it. Oh, it was terrible not to be able to even depend on any sexual interest from him at this moment where he had such little faith in my intelligence. Terrible, that is, not to matter either in substance or spirit. I was ashamed of thinking this way, but other male professors would likely have given me a chance, at least momentarily, trembling as I was there, drenched in my light raincoat. But Lucy did not even invite me to take my things off, any more than he fetched me something to dry myself off with or offered me a cup of tea. He just got right to the point. I needed, now, to think about my thesis. Had I come up with something specific in the field I had chosen? He did not wait for a response but said he had something for me. Then he straightened his legs and inspected his fine leather shoes, a gesture that was a kind of preface to his speech:

Not long ago, one of his colleagues had come across a manuscript related to his particular specialty. The diary of a man who might possibly be the author of several works Lucy had written a little about many years back. He had only taken a glancing look at the manuscript himself, submerged as he was in other projects— "snowed under"—but was quite convinced that the author of the diary, signed only with the initials S. B., would turn out to be the painter S. B., the artist responsible for the famous portrait of Viscount Tom Jones.

Right! Was I supposed to know the portrait? But of course, I nodded, entirely eager, although there was in reality no need for such dissembling in this man's presence; I barely got to open my mouth. I only had to accept the project, which, it went without saying, was a unique opportunity for a young scholar. It wasn't like well-preserved manuscripts from seventeenth century Western Art History grew on trees. Lucy plucked up a little fragment of paper and wrote on it the name and the number of the manuscript. Having done that, he did something I did not expect. He took my hand, smiled and wished me good luck. That farewell was even less convincing than his weak, clammy handshake.

Soon after, I stood outside his building, scrap of paper in hand. The rain had stopped and I decided there was no reason to wait. I was excited to see the manuscript, even if I knew it was a better idea to start by reading something about the work of this S. B. And to clap eyes on the famous painting. Who did he say, Tom Jones? Would I be able to discover what made this work so distinctive? I didn't even know where it was on display.

I had never been to the manuscript library before and was not entirely certain about the system there in the darkness, but soon a friendly young man materialized in front of me, the custodian; before he was able to so much as say good morning, I'd pushed Lucy's fragment of paper at him. "Right," he said, smirking as though he'd half-expected me. I sat on a hard, wooden bench in a dark booth and lit a little lamp attached to a bookshelf in front of the desk. I looked about; there were not many people around.

I was watching a young, focused woman in the neighboring booth when the custodian bustled over and set a brown cardboard box on the desk in front of me. He extended his hands invitingly, and then vanished. I carefully opened the box and took out the book. It was much thicker than I expected, bound in pergament, and considering its age, it was in very good condition. As I opened the book, I wondered if I shouldn't have white gloves on my hands or something. This was all so old and so beautiful. Yes, old, exactly! I stared at the first page and flipped forward. What was this? It was almost as if the lines were collapsing into one another, so cramped were they lying there and filling the pages entirely. And the writing. What had I gotten myself into? I had never learned to read anything like this. Nor had I ever worked with such an old text. I had been reading scholarly articles. First and foremost, I had been reading pictures. As, actually, had Lucy himself. And it was then that I realized why this "great opportunity" had been placed in my hands; he had emphasized getting a copy of my transcript when the work was done. It was clear that I needed help. And that is how I met Mrs. Mary Howard. One of these old, prestigious scholars at the university who had never completed her doctorate.

But it was a grind nonetheless; the result was by and large a poor report of the young artist's daily pottering, since he did not write much about his art. Not until day 203. Then my study took a completely new direction. Day number 203 was not just a remarkable discovery on its own, revealing that S. B. was indeed responsible for the Tom Jones portrait; it changed the manuscript as a whole, for it contained the clue that the author was a woman. What once seemed a petty testimony to everyday, recurrent actions now gained a different meaning; with the aid of a great weight of theoretical material I was able to mine historical significance from almost every word in the manuscript. I drank in everything that had been written about the period, about art and women. And I learned new concepts.

After I delivered Lucy a copy of the transcript, as agreed, I did not have much contact with him. Even my discovery did not change my relationship with him or my status in his eyes. I met him a few times after our first meeting and, of course, told him about what I had been turning up, but he seemed primarily pleased that it was now possible to make clear that the creator of the images he himself had researched was the author of the diary. If I could show that the author and artist was also a woman, that would be truly interesting.

Truly interesting? I thought this lukewarm reaction a bit strange, but Lucy spent much of his time in Spain—the rumor was that he was after a position at the Prado Museum in Madrid—so I concluded that his mind lay there. I decided not to trouble myself and to look for help elsewhere. Old Mary, thanks in fact to Lucy's mediation, was a help to me in everything concerning documentation of the period. I took classes in the gender history and met both teachers and students in relevant areas. Mom followed along with me, insisting on reading everything as I did; during that period, I reckoned she was sending me Amazon shipments at a book a week. All this stuff helped me gain insight and look for clues in S. B.'s text, which was otherwise entirely free from incident. And now the mundanity itself had gained meaning; there was some feminine behavior to that! To these dreary repetitions. The constrained expression. The diarist was holding back. Always "busy around the house." And "in the pantry." And "in the buttery." Eternal headaches, never out of the house unless riding out in the meadows with her father. Never at the tavern. Inconsistent spelling, indicating that the author of the manuscript had not received a formal education. The father the teacher. Always close by. No nudity but great emphasis on patterns in clothing and jewelry. The material of the still life painting was unusual. It was typical of a female artist from the period. But based on various information from the diary, she may have pre-dated all the others, and that made all the difference! Most important, of course, she had created the image of Tom Jones's face that belonged to the art history canon. An image known for its unusual use of color in the face and distinctive depiction of the eyes—the lines around the eyes—an image I now knew as well as my own palm, so often and for such long periods had I looked at and scrutinized it. Indeed, S. B.'s phrasing of the production of the portrait, her connection to it, and the young Jones formed the essence of my thesis: "Every lovely grace of his face." A moment any novelist might well have dreamed could spin out into a memorable story. But here there was no need for the poetic. Documentary testimony to feelings 365 years old was superior to all fiction. But the emphasis on the moment described on day 203 had, of course, not entered my research thanks to some sentimental emotion. The emphasis primarily had theoretical resonance. The moment revealed the story behind an artwork that had a distinctive place among portraits from this era. It gave rise, based on written and personal proof, to a watershed moment in art history from past centuries, one that needed to be heard.

Renaissance Man

"Of course, we have our responsibilities to history." It's my father-in-law speaking, but for what purpose and to whom I am not entirely certain. He's standing in the hallway of our new home, together with his family. The group stands in a knot, somewhat vulnerable, as people always seem once they've slipped off their shoes to enter someone else's home. But who invited these people? And why have they taken off their shoes? It's awful to look at my mother-in-law, in a lightweight outdoor vest which somehow isn't quite an outer garment, in yet more olive-green capris to mark spring, and in thin nylon socks stretched over the bunion at the base of her big toe; she reaches out for me with a warm embrace across her sister-in-law, who seems to have been mid-story, saying something entirely unrelated to my father-in-law's declaration when the visitors arrived. A sister-in-law who is the only one who did not take off her shoes, her heavy, black leather boots that step forcefully along the hallway and almost land on her husband's toe, his white sports socks. He is light-hearted by habit, his thin, fringed hair parted down the middle. Before leaving the house later this evening, he will ask, as usual, for a shoe horn, though he knows full well we do not "hold" with that. After them comes their daughter, seemingly untouched by the environment that fostered her. And she's made of completely different stuff than my father-in-law, who is now in the kitchen, having a little private chat with Hans. No doubt something of great importance.

Next thing, my kitchen is filled with plastic bags and crockery from other houses: common, even crummy, but nonetheless entirely tempting dishes. The party is some kind of potluck that I had no hand in, for which I'd actually tried to avoid being up and about. But when the fragrances meet my appetite, I discover no evident reason to panic; my circumstances will not be mentioned tonight.

The guests seat themselves at the table. I hear conversation but not always what is being said, because my attention is focused on people's gestures and self-presentation. At first, it's my mother-in-law and sister-in-law who do the talking, but as the evening goes by, my father-in-law becomes restless, wanting to present his repertoire. The cultural agenda of the empirical scientist who spends time on serious thought during the day then inclines toward more artistic pursuits in the evening. In his spare time. Perhaps picking up an instrument with some friends. Composing some poetry to be published via an old acquaintance and cultural authority. But what burns within him at this moment has to do with the statement that left his lips as he entered earlier. And since he no longer cares to listen to his son-in-law and his political platitudes, he leans back and takes a meaningful look at us, me and Hans. At the first-rate scientist his son, and his wife, me, who researches ancient images and texts, a subject obscure enough to be somewhat gratifying to him:

"What is your opinion about this Guðlaugur affair?" He appears to direct this question at me in particular, but before I can form any words he continues on with a sort of expansion of the original question, saying in an awkward British accent—a strange thing, given he was educated in America: "Is archival research a special case of the general messiness of life?" Then he squints his eyes down and sets his mouth as though he's planning to answer his own question, first giving me some time to review the case: an esteemed foreign publisher has recently published a significant monograph by a young professor, but now his colleagues in Iceland have drawn attention to the fact that one of the key documents of the research cannot be located where it was said to be kept. And since it does not have its own individual call number, belonging merely to a loosely-catalogued collection, there are doubts about whether the document, a letter from the Foreign Secretary to the American Ambassador, ever actually existed. The young professor believes that the letter has been misplaced and everyone's energy should be put into finding it.

But what exactly was my father-in-law's question? What do I think about the Guðlaugur situation? Or whether archives are inherently jungles, emblematic of life's general chaos? I would likely echo his simile, but then he does something I did not expect anyone to do this evening, and does so in a way that utterly betrays my wishes: "What would happen, for example, if this manuscript you spent so much time researching vanished? Perished. What would happen to your research? Could you still submit your dissertation?"

To make matters more unfortunate, as soon as he lets slip these words, the conversation my mother-in-law and her son-in-law are having about some personal woes of a local councilor up north comes to an end, and so a deadly silence suddenly reigns at the table, causing all the guests look toward me, their coffee cups poised at their lips. Oh, how perfect it would be if my sister-in-law inserted herself into the discussion, wiping out the question that hangs in the air with some tips or buzzword from her field. But she does not do so, and it's actually her daughter who comes to my rescue, breaking the silence with an unexpected, refreshing outburst of well-informed, unprejudiced adolescence, making everyone laugh and bringing the guests together in an unforeseeable, agreeable mood. A mood that does not last though, because soon the sister-in-law comes into her element and railroads everyone. Still, anything is better than my father-in-law's airy meditation about the flat reality of the past, his idea of history; he has reduced me to a pounding heart and cold sweat while he just sits there with the chattering guests. Not able or wanting to join in, he plays with his coffee cup. And once the shoeless guests are milling in a heap in the living room and saying thank you on their way out, I see him standing alone in the hallway. He faces the floor mirror and looks inquiringly at his own image. But what do you need to ask a mirror if you're wearing a stylish sports coat from a popular designer and comfortable corduroy pants ribbed with creases? Stiff creases. "Renaissance man!" Words my old Icelandic teacher spoke about this "versatile" and "talented" father-in-law of mine, who seems to have found the answer to the question his reflection posed, because, sure and certain, he nods his head to himself in the glass as he moves closer to it. Is a poem coming into existence? *Each word must be peised and weighed for valor and wisdom / taking pains over details and progression and systems.* But just when I think he's going to walk clean through the glass, he takes a step backwards, beside the mirror, pulls in his stomach so his chest expands and his face deforms in such a way that his lines deepen, his skin crumples together, and his eyes bulge. Then I see him look toward me. He looks into the mirror and then at my face, reflected there. Just before I turn away.

I pretend to write. Then I start to write.
To write off Diana

I receive a message from Diana D. about needing to discover the little guy. The so-called *Demolitionist*. And I am writing the message down in my notebook when Sigga arrives. We're soon sitting outside on the balcony and are nicely settled there. The balcony is off the dining room, and overlooks the neighboring garden as well as our own, a largely unexplored territory. It suffers from negligence.

"Beautiful," says Sigga, reaching for the notebook, which lies next to my coffee cup on the table between us. She caresses the string, but instead of opening it, as she seems to have planned, she places the bright pink leather object in my outstretched palm and says, "You're better, aren't you? Could you get some help wrapping things up?"

Sigga would understand me, she would do anything for me in this hopeless situation in which I've found myself, but nothing can help me. My problem is such that it can only worsen if I drag it into daylight: "Yes, but there are things I'm not entirely satisfied with."

"Did you know that the loft attic in that house is full of old dolls?" She indicates the old Danish stone house next door. I make a mock ghostly sound and say there's nothing sinister about such stereotyped and worn out symbols, that they can't possibly arouse fear in anyone.

"Still, it would be fascinating to know more," she says, draining her cup; she has to go to another meeting at the manufacturing plant, safety helmet firmly on her head, to discuss something I know nothing about. This oldest, dearest friend of mine. Who has a fierce passion for nineteenth century English literature and everything connected to it but who, due to a series of chances, of wrong decisions, has to waste her days as far away from that world as possible. She was an outstanding student, equally competent in all her subjects in school, and so no one ever thought anything except that she would go on to study science. But in high school she met the fateful jerk who did nothing but humiliate her with troubling, underhanded behavior. Still, nothing seemed to be able to dampen her affection for her boyfriend, and eventually she followed him on to university where she achieved such distinction that she was offered a grant for graduate study abroad, which she had no choice but to accept, because at that point the boy had finally put an end to their relationship, and her only desire was to flee the country. And now Sigga Daðadóttir makes hay from this great education with endless high-paid work opportunities and a sweet husband educated in the same field. But she rarely speaks about her job and the place she is trapped because to do so would bring back to mind the humiliation of high school and her loss of self-respect.

Sigga reminds me of our planned trip to her parents' cabin before she walks herself to the door. I sit a while longer on the balcony with my notebook. At the top of the first page I have written: *Meeting with Diana D. May 30 at 14:00. Notes about the Demolitionist.* Why had I not yet canceled? Was I looking for the perfect excuse so that it would not be possible to be read into the cancellation, or use it against me to indicate that I really did need help? I close the book, hold it up to my face and run the tip of my nose along the leather. Then I see the woman. I first noticed her the other day. She'd had her back to me and was patching something in the house. Now she's out in the spring air, straw hat on her head, wearing loose clothes and gardening gloves. She rummages in the flower beds, her face hidden under the hat, but when she stands up, I see she's an old, thin woman. Almost emaciated.

The south wind moves the clouds from the sun. I lean back in my chair, eyes closed behind dark sunglasses, feet on the balcony rail. When the heat is about to seal itself around me the clouds come floating back. I jerk my feet toward myself and am about to head inside when I see the gardening woman standing up close to the limestone wall separating our two gardens. She looks right at me, but I barely get to notice her face, because I instinctively look down into my lap and go momentarily stock still. Since I feel I cannot hold the position anymore, though I also can't look up, I reach for my notebook. I pretend to write. Then I start to write. To write off Diana. A quick reflection in the form of questions that I end up responding to with another reflection. A reflection about the *Demolitionist.* Then I pretend to read over my words just before I get up and head inside.

I want to call Sigga and ask her where she heard the story about the attic dolls. I know she will pick up the phone as she stands in her suit-skirt amid a swarm of guys inside the colossal plant, saying, "Excuse me a moment, I have to take this." But I don't call, because my phone rings instead; it's Hans, letting me know he will be late, so I ask him if he knows anything about the woman in the house behind us, though I know he does not. I put the notebook on the coffee table and throw myself down on the couch. I lie there with eyes wide open, fearful of seeing what I almost just saw, and would see if I close them. I look at the door behind the tapestry until my eyes grow heavy. And then she appears. The gardening woman. Standing beside the tapestry, arrow-straight and resting her pitchfork on the floor. She looks straight ahead.

And it's Bonný who breaks the silence,
raising the question of whether this all has
anything to do with the professor

I had insisted on being unable to attend the cabin getaway but
was having second thoughts. And in my head, there's a memory,
an image of a grassy patch by a little hollow. Of a teak sofa with
a moss-green woolen cover, facing a table of the same wood with
storage for magazines under the leaf; the two of us sitting there.
Eleven years old. Short-haired, wearing tight turtleneck shirts
and striped toe-socks. We let ourselves sink down into the thin,
loose cushion. It's hard underneath and unstable but we don't
think about this with our faces behind the *Weekly News*. I read
about the mysterious experiences of some Icelanders during this
era of space travel, while Sigga reads about going to the moon.
Why send a man to the moon without being sure he can return?
Then she stands up, puts the magazine on the table, where it falls
open to the French president and the great power he seems to
have over his surroundings, and says she wants to go outside. But
I'm too absorbed in the story of Aron Guðbrandsson, the Stock
Exchange Director, concerning a mysterious incident that took
place in his office in the center of Reykjavík in the mid-1960s.

I'm finishing Aron's story when Sigga's father, Daði, gets out of
the bathroom, for sure having just peed a little bit on the peach-
colored, downy-soft and fluffy contour mat, having dried his
strong, coarse hands on a mint-green hand towel and tucking it,
according to the custom of the house, in the flowery copper ring
so that the embroidered water lily and the lace edge face out. Tall
and robust, he carefully closes the door and walks toward me. For
some reason, I flip further on in the magazine, past the mysterious
experience of the speculator, and once Daði is standing by the
sofa where I'm sitting, magazine in hand, he looks down at me,
claps me on the back, and laughs at the comic strip: "Mr. Jiggs."
Then he's out on the terrace looking down at the water. I reach
toward and rifle about in the pile of magazines, which seem at
first glance to be somewhat older than the cabin itself. On the
cover of one is a sketch of a young girl with a notebook in front
of her. The girl rests her cheek in her hand and gazes off thoughtfully on December 15, 1938. I look at an article about a Spanish
painter who despises his fans; I grab another issue and am about
to start reading a story called "The Luncheon" when I hear my
name called from the terrace. It's Daði, smiling there outside and
pointing toward the lake to indicate that I should come out and
join them on a trip down there.

   I do not get up right away, but look at him from the living
room, as he first takes off his delicate slippers then puts on black
rubber boots. I'm thinking about where this man came from and
how he became the way he is. How is he so gentle and tender,
having been raised by a single father in a remote region? About
how my own father is also such a good man. So warm and just
and almost unbearably tolerant for having grown up in a cramped,

damp place with seven siblings and two apathetic parents in Reykjavík in the middle of last century.

No, I did not ask about any of this back then. I'm asking myself
now, lying in bed in my new home in Reykjavík with Hans's breath
in my ears, and later I ask: Where are all those old *Weekly News*es
now? Were they thrown in the trash at the end of the century, or
are they at the bottom of some new storage compartment, hidden
under a beech table-leaf that closes up and which has replaced
the old teak table? Are they lying there under some new gloss-
ies? Under the gleaming but depressing pictures Bjarnfríður Una
starts to rummage through with one of her large paws—the other
holding a beer can—the day all the women except me arrive at the
cabin, having hardly finished taking stuff out of their cars. Bjarnfríður Una sits down in a brown wicker chair, sets the can down
on the pulled-out table leaf, and fishes out from the storage sec-
tion a recent magazine that includes, among other things, twenty
photographs of a British television star and her lesser-known lover
in various places within their cheerless, tidy home; Queen Eliza
beth in a red coat and a hat of the same color, then an ash-gray
coat with blue hat, a salmon pink coat with olive-green hat, a
dark purple coat with golden-brown hat, a magenta-red coat with
white hat, a siren-pink coat with purple-colored feathers on her
head, a pale yellow coat with scarlet red hat, a plum-colored dress
with a fuchsia pillbox on her head, a coral hat and an indigo blue
dress, a lime coat with a hat completely in style, and bending her
head and looking down at the earth.

I can picture Bjarnfríður examining these peculiar images, all
without considering the historical context the captions provide,
the tiny letters she doesn't read beside the hugely stretched, shiny

photographs, no different from the rest of the magazine's millions of readers around the world.

I lie awake, eyes closed. I know my friends are not yet going to bed; they'll be sitting up in the paneled living room. Flames in the fireplace. On the dining table, candlelight and red wine in glasses. Whose idea had this trip been? Are they talking about me right now? Shouldn't they be asking themselves what's up with my thesis; most of them must know I should have finished two months ago? Bonný immediately comes to my defense and explains, in the manner of scholars, that the final sprint can be almost everlasting, while Ester wonders aloud whether I've been gone four or five years, Sigga A. says it's been six, Sigga D. considers that normal, Tína thinks it likely that our homecoming is to do with Hans's job, Bjarnfríður Una asks about the grant from the British Embassy and, in addition, but just briefly, about the student loan, Sigga D. emphasizes that I have come home because of illness, Bjarnfríður Una says that I have been as fit as a fiddle these past days, Tína that I have in fact been a bit, a tiny bit, distracted, Ester: "Nonsense," Tína points out that Hans is the dominant one in the relationship, Bonný mentions my mother in connection with all this. "Huh?" Ester responds, "Why would the mother want her daughter home before finishing?" Silence. Until Bjarnfríður declares that it is important for me to "land" my thesis after what she calls my "artistic fiasco," which startles me; Bonný reacts, too, moralizing in response to Bjarnfríður's words; meanwhile, Guðbjörg is not quite sure what I have been studying. Another silence, longer than the previous. And it's Bonný who breaks it, raising the question of whether this all has anything to do with the professor. It's as though the group has been given a command from on high. They all look down at the table and take

in Bonný's suspicion, nodding their heads. All in line until Sigga
D. declares that whatever may have happened to my thesis, it is
likely to be a major breakthrough. Yes, Bonný says, she's heard
that too. And then they all look at each other and keep nodding.
Everyone except Bjarnfríður Una: "Heard?"

No, it's rather unlikely that such a conversation is taking place
at the cabin. More probably, something like this is going on: Ester
has drunk the most, Tína hot on her heels; Sigga A. has drunk
nothing because she is driving home tonight. Ester's swift gulps
probably gave rise to the discussion around the table about her
own circumstances back home in the suburbs. Namely, that not
so long ago her husband, the coach, had not spoken a word for
three days after some loss in some tournament, and Tína does
not consider the situation acceptable. Ester at first defends her
husband, but the more she drinks the more she gives up and
admits that this damn ball game has overbalanced her marriage
and domestic life. Worse is the constant imbalance between disap
pointment and bottomless euphoria.

"Isn't the worst thing that this self-obsessed ex-sportsman,
who couldn't even be at the birth of his youngest son because of
some game, has gotten obese?" I ask myself and roll over onto
my other side. But of course, no one at the table can take note of
my words from where I am lying alongside the calm, low, almost
delicate snoring of Hans up against my right ear. On the contrary,
it's Bjarnfríður Una who steps up to the plate on behalf of the
sports fanatic. Maybe to spite Tína. But everything settles down,
as usual, and now that they've moved into the living room, I can
picture Ester under a blanket with some Pepsi in a glass. She seems
distracted. Bjarnfríður Una, however, has some political argument
in preparation, following on from something said earlier, and this

causes Guðbjörg and Bonný to go off and talk privately together. Sigga A. is, for her part, heading out. And after she has let the door bang shut behind her and disappeared into the darkness, headed through the underpass back to the city, back to the outskirts, back to a street with a strange name, back through the door of her modern white house, that box, back into the large, empty hallway where she will put her car keys on a metal table with glass top, a console table under the contemporary and colorful amateur abstract, while the heir to the cabin, Sigga D., suggests a game. That's well received and Sigga goes into her parents' room and fetches a board game that is kept in the upper bunk alongside other items meant for amusing oneself at the cottage. It's the bunk across from her parents' double bed where the old oversize doll still sits, a bizarre décor from the early seventies stretching out its arms toward patient Daði, who constantly had to remove it when he lay down to rest in the middle of the day in the rural peace and quiet, flopping his big, sturdy body on a shiny, smooth blanket.

Sigga sets a trivia board game on the table and I realize I am not going to fall asleep easily. Ester's going to play, too. Tína puts her arms around her, and Bjarnfríður, who hadn't been especially enthusiastic about the idea, plunks herself down beside them on a soft, bulky corner sofa, light blue, pale pink, dark burgundy, light gray, dark gray, moss green, forest green and beige. She lifts her beer glass to toast her friends, as though she's trying to signal that a new chapter in this little trip is about to begin. Let's roll the dice.

The first question of the night is a geography one; it's Sigga D. who asks Bjarnfríður, "What is the name of the canyon inland between Högnhöfði and Rauðafell . . . ?"

"Brúarárskörð," blurts out the political candidate, reaching for a blue wedge that she slips into the wheel, where it sits fast once her rough forefinger has tamped it down, as if to emphasize her knowledge, how she has already taken the lead. And she is so proud of her answer that she doesn't realize the next question is also hers to answer: "Who was the leader of the Puritans in the Civil War in England, 1642 to 1651?"

The sound Bjarnfríður Una emits is meant to indicate the name has slipped her mind. She takes a big swig of beer to buy some time, but it's no use because she doesn't know the answer, evident enough from the expression on Tína's face; she rolls her eyes as she names the commander.

Ester's turn. "Who became Icelandic men's handball champions in 2010?" The suburbanite is all excited because she knows the answer, and she's zealously embraced by her girlfriends as she drops an orange pie into her wheel. She rolls the die again, ready for another category. "What year was Elizabeth II crowned British queen?"

"I don't care," says Ester, deciding to start talking about the surreal absurdist—that's the influence of Guðbjörg, the realtor—that is crowns and scepters, but Tína sets down her empty red wine glass to point out that one does not have to watch history through the moralistic glasses of the contemporary moment, that such events have inherent interest due to their symbolism, their historical context, and . . .

Tína doesn't get to finish because Bjarnfríður Una, evidently indifferent to her monologue, has drawn a card and directs the question to Sigga: "What French writer is the author of these words: *Everything leads us to believe that there exists a spot in the*

mind where the real and the imaginary cease to appear contradictory?"
She squints her eyes to read the card and answer silently to herself.

Sigga does not have the answer, and Bjarnfríður does not provide
the French name, instead turning to the next question, directing it
to Tína. Bjarnfríður looks at the card, glancing up in astonishment:
"What famous novelist always addressed his mother as a man?"

"Bjarnfríður, I'm on a yellow square." Bjarnfríður Una begs
Tína's apology with a solemn gesture and looks back on the card.
And she smiles: "Who was the first woman to serve as the speaker
of the Icelandic parliament?"

"First woman what? What does it matter?"

"I don't know whether it matters, but I would have thought
you, of all of us, would consider it a duty for every Icelander to
know it."

"A duty," Tína replies, in a whisper; suddenly, her voice rises:
"Is this some duty? For which Icelanders?"

Buna holds ten stubby fingers up in the air, trying to calm
Tína, who now stands up and weaves a course into the bathroom.
She firmly closes the door behind her, walks toward the sink,
closes both hands around the rim and looks into the mirror, on a
perfumed, heart-shaped pillow with lace trim that hangs from a
wicker shelf full of cosmetics, old and new; beside it there's a white
plastic shelf, also full of massive bottles of laundry detergent. And
behind them lies a rolled-up blue cloth. In the mirror, behind
the despairing face of this self-scrutinizing, endlessly-searching
humanist, a few toilet rolls can be seen in their hand-sewn dis-
pensers; each roll has been placed in an embroidered fabric cylin-
der, though the patterns are hard to discern in the mirror.

"I do not remember the woman's name," says Ester, from
the other side of the partition, and Guðbjörg, who, like Bonný,

is not playing, agrees with a shrug of her shoulders; just when Bjarnfríður is about to school her friends on the importance of this office, Tína comes storming into the living room. She has the blue roll from the white bathroom shelf in her hand. She stands in front of Bjarnfríður, unrolls the material, and holds it up in front of her face: "Do you know what this is?"

Bjarnfríður leans back in the soft and dimly-colored seat, placid as water and rather clearer-voiced than the amount of beer she's imbibed would suggest: "I believe it's the Icelandic flag. The symbol of our country and nation."

"You can call it whatever you want," says the actress, and with some force; she brandishes the flag at her side like she's a matador: "but when all is said and done, it's nothing but a tricolor scrap of fabric used to brainwash people like you!" Tína crumples the material and is about to drop it on the dining table, but suddenly stops and reaches for a white slip of paper that dropped onto the floor as soon as she raised the flag in the air. "No, this won't do," she mumbles, tearing open the folded note and reading, and then suddenly saying, loud and clear: "*If the flag gets wet, it should not be folded and put away to store before it has had time to dry.* Listen to that! Not before it's had time to dry!" Then she throws it down on the table, curses, gives a hollow laugh and, as she tries to yank open the handle on the door to the terrace, bumps herself against an embroidered wall-hanging beside the door, onto which countless buttons from charities and organizations have been pinned; the hanging sways like a pendulum in a clock, almost knocking into some wine bottles that seem to hover, horizontal, on the wall, where they have been for some time now, ever since Sigga D. and her siblings gave her teetotal parents this futuristic wine rack. And the wall-hanging is still in motion on the wall by the time Tína is out on the terrace lighting herself a cigarette and Sigga Daðadóttir takes her father's flag off the table and folds it like a tablecloth.

In the meanwhile, Bonný has gone into her room, flung herself down on her bed with her phone, and sent her friend, that is, me, the one left behind in Reykjavík, this message: *You are missing a lot, hon*! Bonný puts the phone away and looks at the paneling above her head. Then she retrieves the phone and continues writing. She writes for some time. Her thumbs seem unstoppable.

But even if my phone had been switched on at that moment, I would not have heard the pings: I'm under my blanket on my way to sleep with Hans's bass snoring in my right ear. I know I am because my innermost thoughts no longer entirely cohere. The last one I have is the welcome fact that I will not have to wake up with my friends tomorrow morning. Wish them good morning in that country cottage which Time, with all its tasteless junk, has so ill-treated.

I have no sooner rejoiced at my absence from the cottage than I'm startled by a loud crash right above me. I open my eyes and try to sit up but am obstructed and get nowhere. I lie back on my pillow and reach my hand up into the darkness. There are wooden planks above me, but the scant brightness that now slips into the room prevents me from believing for a moment that I am enclosed inside a coffin. In the distance, I hear whispers, then laughter, but low. Then silence.

I look around. Below the boards I see red. On the wall at my feet hangs a picture. Two gypsies in red dresses dancing. Flamenco. In the background burns a fire. I know this picture. I have looked at it in the dark, it has appeared in my dreams, it has watched me and bid me good morning. And never has such a day failed me.

This picture, presumably full of tragic and sorrow, calls forth a foggy memory about the endless joy of careless youth. But as soon as I try to figure out that memory, the image dissolves and once again there is nothing but red. I wipe my tears and try to remember where I've seen it before. Then I hear birdsong, then snoring, directly above me. I crawl out from under the boards to see who it is. In a bunk opposite the bed lies someone wearing an eye mask. I look back at the wall. The two gypsies. I hear laughter again, but not in the distance like before. Now the figure tosses and turns in reaction to the sounds. I see who it is. It's Bjarnfríður Una.

I get out of bed and walk to the door. I open it gently and peep out the crack. I can smell coffee. Then I hear Sigga's laughter, Bonný's whispering. I close the door and am planning to throw myself back into bed and go back to sleep and so go straight to Reykjavík, but it does not seem possible, because by now Bjarnfríður's arm is dangling all the way down from the edge of the bunk, preventing me from getting back in. I take her palm, her stubby fingers and well-groomed nails, varnished but clipped, and try to somehow tuck the arm back onto the bunk; as I do, the door opens behind me.

"Good morning!" says Sigga, lively but not too loud.

They come together, one after another, emerging from their rooms, and there's no evidence last night's events are going to linger. Not one word about Bjarnfríður and Tína's conflict; they seem in the best of moods. After morning coffee, it's decided we should go for a walk.

We drive to the valley off the big fjord. We leave the cars and walk through the small canyon to a river across which lies a tree trunk. Ester goes over first with all the certainty of someone responsible for others. Tína tiptoes behind her, then Bjarnfríður

Una who almost slips off the trunk, asking whether there wasn't once a rope for supporting oneself. Bonný and Guðbjörg and Sigga follow. I'm last.

We head along the river. Toward the waterfall. Along the path for about half an hour until we're treading on unstable ground, it feels almost like it's breaking apart. We walk out onto the cliffs and see a good two hundred meters of waterfall down into the narrow gorge. But we can't see the whole waterfall so Sigga and Tína inch us out onto the edge of the cliff, which drops down a little. I go ahead, lying on my stomach, and they are right behind me.

The sun is so high that the rays reach the far end of the canyon. Through the sparkling foam, I think I can see a gleam in the bottom if I shift myself closer to the edge. The girls do not stir; they are squatting down. Then I hear someone shout, wondering whether we should really keep going. It's Ester. I place my palms on the ground and am getting to my feet when my right foot slips on a rock and I slide down, toppling onto my rear over the edge of the cliff and scrabbling at the surface, which is nothing but loose stones, I cannot get myself back up.

I give out a choked cry and at once they're all beside the cliff's edge. Sigga reaches her hand toward me, while Tína holds onto her hips. Bonný and Ester are behind them, and I think they're holding onto Tína who orders them to go back because she needs to get a better grip on Sigga. I cannot see Guðbjörg as I stretch my hand toward Sigga and Tína, but behind the group, somewhat above them, Bjarnfríður Una stands out against the sky. She seems stiff, not exactly out of fear, more on account of something that looks like worry. Worry about her own reaction at this moment? Or some anxiety connected to wider issues arising from this crisis? As though she is thinking of the fallout, of how I'll slip further down and finally fall into the gorge; as though she is deliberating who would be responsible. Trying to assess what my curiosity will cost the group? Society? And now I feel like I recall Ester and the others' conversation a moment ago when walking up the hill, a conversation about an accident that occurred at an altogether different place in another ravine where a foreign couple were traveling ten years or so ago. What had happened? Did the woman fall into the canyon? Did she survive the fall? Was she found? I did not catch it all, all I can say is that people searched for her over several days; riffing off that fact, they, or rather Bjarnfríður, started to talk about travel insurance and other similar things while I tried not to hear but still did. And now I realize that Bjarnfríður is mulling over her words as she stands back from the cliff edge, and this causes her face to deform. And the smile that now moves across it is thin and strained; I've been tugged back up to the top and collapse into the arms of Sigga, around whom Tína's arms reach, and so on and so forth.

With tears in our eyes but still laughing, we walk away from the waterfall. From there we go back across the river and down to the cars. We do not discuss my slip further, but Bjarnfríður Una avoids meeting my glance for the rest of the trip.

How often can you go over and over a dream in your mind until the scenario begins to crack apart, its images crumbling, their lifetime becoming nothing more than the moment it takes to call them up? I lift myself up from my pillow with the image of a landscape in my head: a cliff gully in appalling brightness. Then I lie back with a strange lightness in my heart, not really knowing why, as the landscape runs together with the first thought of the day. And is thereby forever gone.

Flipping through, my thumb on the fore edge. Again and again. I reckon that one out of every three times the pages fall in such a way that the book opens where my secret lies

"The difficulty with this kind of management is of course integrating the practical aspects with those that bow to development and the artistic vision." Trees form a frame around the face in the glass sphere so it appears bigger than the rest of the body. Mom is wearing a cream-colored shirt beneath a dark-blue woolen jacket, her hair silver gray and impeccable as ever. She looks around, steps a little closer, and when she reaches the door she looks straight into the peephole. Now I don't dare open it for her, for fear she'll fall directly in through the door; I simply look right into her eyes as she reiterates what she just said: "The hardest thing about this kind of management is taking part in shaping the field while at the same time serving those who actually lead the changes." She has come straight from a board meeting at the Art Museum.

As she asks me how my headache is, she turns away and installs herself at the fridge. Notices the conference program fixed to the fridge door with a magnet on which is written:

*Close some doors today. Not because of pride,
incapacity, or arrogance, but simply because they
lead you nowhere.*

"Oh." And from the movement of her nape I can tell Mom is
rolling her eyes as she follows the saying. Then she looks down
into an earthenware bowl with paper clips, small change, and used
batteries. Into which I had tossed this fridge magnet my sister-in-
law brought me with these words from her favorite author. Out of
which Hans had retrieved it, entirely without thought, and used it
to remind himself about an upcoming conference.

As if to brush away the wisdom on the fridge, Mom begins
to talk about a group exhibition by some Nordic artists, which
reminds her of the latest installation at the museum, and that
brings her yet again to the newly installed exhibition by the afore-
mentioned promising young mirror artist. But at that moment the
coffeepot starts beeping, almost as if blowing a fulltime whistle
to end her speech about the mirror-woman. And somehow—for-
tunately—that makes it difficult for Mom to pick up the thread
again once we sit down at the kitchen table.

In the silence she looks into the air. At the ceiling. At the cracks
that have formed there in the corner. Reaching along to the wall
and down to the kitchen floor, toward a black discoloration on
the floor, and she repeats her and Dad's offer to assist us in buying
a home. Dr. Theodor had not been in any position to maintain
the home after his wife died, and everything needs ripping out
and starting over.

Mom gets up and tells me she's going to use the bathroom.
As soon as she closes the door, I recall my one visit to this house.
I wouldn't even have been nine years old, but I remember it all,

even if rather hazily. My mother was there with me; just the doctor's wife was at home. They—the two doctor's wives—were sitting in the kitchen; I waited for Mom in the hall by the entryway. I sat on some sort of bench that had a table affixed to it, looking through the half-open door opposite me. It was the door down to the basement. Staring through, I thought I saw something moving inside. I got up and went to check it out. When I pushed the door further ajar, I found a mural painted on the curved wall that descended with the stairs, women and men holding hands like they were walking downstairs. From their faces, one could assume that they were in the thrall of some kind of joy; some of them actually seemed to be witless with pleasure, and it made me scared but also a little excited. The picture covered the entire wall, and continued around the corner, so it was tempting to go down and see where the single file of people ended. But then I heard Mom behind me, and knew we were leaving. As I closed the door again, the lady looked at me with a wide smile, really a broad grin, and I understood immediately from that expression that she was referencing the wall people. That's how I knew the image was actually there. And probably still is, under the light-green paint now covering the wall beside the steps down to the basement.

But what had they talked about in the kitchen, the two women? Most likely, thinking of it now, it was related to the daughter, my Mom's childhood girlfriend. Hrefna The. She had gone abroad to study art and never returned, far as I knew. Perhaps that absence, and the silence about her, had everything to do with her dissolute life. That's how I remember it.

When Mom comes back from the toilet, I ask her about Hrefna. Where she ended up, this old friend who negotiated from abroad a way for us to live in the apartment after we came back to Iceland. Mom claims to know almost nothing; she looks out the kitchen window. She gets up and moves over to it. Through the glass, I see the gardening woman briefly appear in her living room window. She vanishes and reappears. Like she's walking in circles. About to ask Mom if she knows anything about this woman, I realize it's not her she's been watching. Mom is looking out into the garden. Dandelions cover the overgrown lawn, but in the midst of the negligence glints some rusty iron trash. I think it's an old lawn mower. I look at Mom. She shakes her head, and I think it's likely over something concerning Dr. Theodor's last few years here in the house. Then she goes into the living room; I'm left behind in the kitchen.

Why do I have a headache, Mom? Why don't you ask about it? I ask myself as I stand at the kitchen door and look through the dining room and into the room where Mom stands at the table. She's holding a book and I see now it's the one from the bottom of the heap on the table: *Sex, Gender, and Subordination in Early Modern England*. One of her first Amazon shipments. She rests her thumb on the fore edge and lets the pages fall from her fingers one after another. I'm about to rush over to her but instead retreat into the kitchen. I bang my head against the wall and try to make up my mind whether or not I should try to stop what might be about to happen, but by the time I'm ready to rush back into the living room and rip the book from her hands, she has put it back on the table. She looks at me, smiling but worried. Almost as sad as when she says goodbye to me.

It's probably about an hour since she left. I'm sitting on the couch with the book in my hand. *Sex, Gender* and all that. Flipping through, my thumb on the fore edge. Again and again. I reckon that one out of every three times the pages fall in such a way that the book opens where my secret lies. A one-third probability that Mom saw the page removed from one book and hidden in the middle of this other book; a greater probability she immediately realized where that page comes from. But I cannot know for sure. I take out the loose page and do what I know I should not do. I fold it in half and slip it inside my notebook, in the pocket inside the cover. Snap the golden elastic.

I no longer know if I'm watching or imagining what's in front of me

I take decisive steps out the alley, but once I'm back on the street, I stop suddenly. This probably isn't a good idea. I turn around, bolt back, lift the lid off the trash can and am rummaging about in the rotting fruit and other food scraps when someone rubs my head gently and whispers: "I'm going. Your mother rang last night after you fell asleep."

I push away any thoughts about her reason for calling and get out of bed. I'm sitting on the living room sofa. I look at the computer screen in front of me. No email from Lucy. He seems to have decided to no longer be part of my existence. That's his problem, but on the other hand there's a missive from a woman who's trying very hard to be part of my world. This is the afore-mentioned Diana D. The message is further preparation for our first meeting, which is almost upon us, without any real awareness of it on my part, and thanks to my sister-in-law's arrangement. To the *Demolitionist* assignment has now been added what the coach calls *unnecessary baggage*. Something it is imperative to get rid of before continuing on the *path*.

But I'm not going along any *path*. I'm not going anywhere. And although my difficulty is possibly, according to the metaphorical language of this dabbler, a kind of "baggage," I'm not sure whether or not to accurately term it "unnecessary." Nor is this baggage one I really pull behind me. It's more like I push it ahead of me, since if I don't do that I'd be forced to have it in tow indefinitely and such a thought is unbearable. What alternative would Diana D. propose for me in these circumstances? Thinking outside the box? But what box? The container that holds the manuscript? That brown case the young custodian never tired of setting on the table in front of me every single day for over a year? No, I'll probably never escape out of that box.

I close my laptop. To be honest: I slam it shut. And the doorbell rings. The evangelicals? Again? I stand up and walk toward the door. But as I put my hand on the knob, I pressed my eye to the peephole. Mom. So early? That can only mean one thing. It's up. She's here to interrogate me!

I carefully let go of the knob and back away from the door, into the living room. I sit on the couch, leaning myself down on one arm to make sure I cannot be seen through the window. I know I should get back on my feet and open up for her but I just cannot shift myself and when she begins to knock on the door, it's as if I'm paralyzed. But she will soon conclude I have gone on a morning stroll.

When I think sufficient time has passed, I get up from the couch. I'm headed toward the hallway to ascertain whether she's really gone when I hear a key being put in the lock. That blows me away for a moment; I'm more afraid than angry. I look around and before I know it I have put my hand under the tapestry, opened the door and pulled myself inside. And I dare not close it because Mom is now coming inside. She stands a short moment in the hallway, then walks very deliberately into the living room. I push the door open a few millimeters and look out across the living room floor. Her well-made, sensible footwear gives me a shocking fright: cognac-brown loafers with pebbled rubber soles that curl up over the heel. Designed to spare the leather when one's foot is on the gas pedal in a shiny new car. Mom stands in the middle of the room and looks around. I see now she has her arms full of stuff. I pull myself further back from the crack and lean against the far wall. I'm not really thinking, just drawing deep, fast breaths. Then I peek again. She has gone up to the window. She is fitting new curtains. As she promised.

There's nothing I can do but sit against the wall and wait. After a while I move toward the cracked door again. The living room is in darkness behind the thick curtains, but Mom is still there. I see her shape as she sits on the couch and looks around. Then she leans across and strokes the lid of my computer. She stands up, but before she walks away from the table she reaches down to the sofa and fetches something lying there on the cushion. My notebook. She has it gripped between her thumb and forefinger and strikes it firmly against her other palm. Just when I think she's about to release the golden elastic and open the book, she looks straight ahead. And before I manage to close the door all the way again, I see her looking in my direction. She takes some steps this way, approaching quite close, making me throw myself back from the gap in the door, pressing myself up against the wall, trying to vanish. I close my eyes and cover my ears, but that does not prevent me from hearing her take hold of the handle. I push my hands still tighter against my ears but nonetheless hear when she closes the door. I feel I can almost hear her adjust the tapestry and smooth it out against the wall.

I lie on the floor in the dark and listen to my rapid heartbeats in cold silence. A mild pulsating starts up inside my head. I know I have to get out of here and get my medicine but I cannot be sure Mom is gone. I won't move until I've heard her close the front door again. I hold my head and hope for the best.

Within the darkness I hear a sound. A hum that little by little turns into a singing voice. It sounds faint and far away. I hear it as a recording. The voice is high, but there's a hum in the recording that muddies the quiet accompaniment via clicks that beat fast like the spatter of frying butter in a pan. It sounds like an old recording. I open my eyes and look up but there's nothing. On the wall opposite the door I see the gold frame hanging. But it is much further away from me now than before; the room is much bigger than before. I stand up and sense something brush my shoulder, but when I feel about behind me there's nothing.

I move toward the frame. It takes approximately five steps. My movements are reflected in the glass. But it's not a mirror. There's a picture behind the glass. And when I squint, I see it a little better. A thin countenance framed in shoulder-length, dark brown, wavy locks, a lace-trimmed collar on a black dress: *Tudor and Jacobean Portraits. September 2-August 3 19*. A poster from an art museum.

I bend down and press my face against the glass to better ascertain the date, but it's like the characters shift. I put my hand on the glass and get to my feet and back away a few steps. Something inside the image moves. In the dark background of the poster, behind the young man's visage, someone is standing. I have to make up my mind what the devil is happening, because otherwise I'll go mad from fear. But I may already have done so: what moves inside the picture is not behind the glass. It's reflected in the glass. It's standing behind me.

I stand still as a grave and look ever so cautiously behind me. But there's no one. Just darkness. I look back at the glass. More movement. And now I see what it is. A woman. She's in profile, standing straight as an arrow, arms by her sides, and in one hand she holds a handbag. The picture of the young man, the artwork, against the wall, begins to dissolve, the background comes to the surface, and I can now see that opposite the woman is a man sitting in a deep chair. Seen from my perspective, he is behind her, and so I cannot make out the foot of one of his crossed legs; suddenly his other leg swings across, alternately disappearing and reappearing from behind the woman, who is standing by a dining table. She has put her bag on the table and seems to be looking for something inside. Sometimes she makes a shooing motion with one hand; now and then something or someone outside the frame pulls at her dress. A shining shirtwaist dress. One that gleams and shines. She moves slightly to one side. With that, two things happen at once: the singing voice falls silent and I can see the man more fully. His face is still hidden behind the newspaper he is reading, but when I squint my eyes, the image becomes so impossibly clear that I can make out on the front page a large photograph: crowds gathered around a clock. I no longer know if I'm watching or imagining what's appearing to me, but it seems to me that it could be the same shabby clock that has always been in the center of Reykjavík, used as both timekeeper and billboard. I cannot read the little letters beneath the picture, but the news headline suggests that about twenty-five thousand people are gathered here. At the bottom of this same page there's another article. The start of the headline is hidden behind the man's finger, but it finishes with: "Peace finally in the Middle East." I measure these words against the photo of Reykjavík, the man's timeless tweed, and the woman's morning frock. But before I can get anywhere with those thoughts the woman walks across the picture and passes out of it. Then the man gets up from where he is reading; he looks toward the bottom corner of the image at something moving there. He lets go of the newspaper, without looking ahead, and slips out of the chair. He gets on all fours. He crawls across the living room floor. And out of the picture.

I tap on the glass but jerk my hand back when she reappears, the woman in the shirtwaist dress. Not from beneath the frame where she disappeared, but rather from inside the glass: she appears in the middle of the picture and turns to me but I cannot see her face, she half-conceals it, she shakes her head and turns to head out to the corner of the picture where the man crawled away. There she throws down her bag and lets herself fall to the floor; immediately she gets up again and heads straight ahead as though she's going to emerge from the glass toward me with open arms. I look away and turn back but collide with some fabric, the white material I had seen hanging from the ceiling a few days earlier and felt brush my shoulder when I stood up from the floor a while ago. When I flail for the door handle I feel something gently touch my face. It's a hand, and now it's about to covers my eyes. Not from behind, but rather from the side, one palm on my face, the other on my neck. I try to break free, to tear the hand from my face, to knock it away from me with as much force as possible. But I achieve nothing, just beat at the soft fabric in front of me, which swings to and fro, away and back. I push the material aside to get closer to the door, but there's no way past it, I seem to be trapped in here in some kind of tent; I lie down on the floor and try to crawl toward the door. But I cannot get out because now some slender hands have gripped me around the waist, someone tries to pull me back into the room. I cannot shake off the grip even though I kick out but I still somehow manage to stretch a hand up and grab the handle. But just as I mean to throw the door open and crawl into the apartment, I hear a familiar voice from the living room. I want to call for help, but hesitate for a moment, pulling the door to again, because now I'm not at all sure what is what.

"You sly old devil!" The words resound from the other side of the door, and at that very moment the grip on my waist is released. The ambassador of the ordinary, my sister-in-law's husband, has exorcised the drivel in my head with these four words. Words he's often used before in friendly ways, thoughtlessly. Unlike on this occasion: "I've come straight from the university, from a seminar held on account of the visit of a political scientist from Denmark. But where's your wife?"

"I'm not exactly sure," says Hans as he walks into the narrow crack that has now formed between the open door and the frame; he sits on the sofa, opposite his brother-in-law.

"Well, it's not always easy to tell, is it? Where our women go off to," the uninvited guest replies, laughing: "Or what they're getting *up* to." Hans nods his head, less convinced than he should really be considering that I'm hiding behind the door.

Hans's brother-in-law inhales and I see in Hans's face that he does not want to take part in the imminent private conversation. "Let me tell you, your sister, though she's an expert in human behavior, is hardly the easiest person to be married to." The lecturer has clearly had a few drinks.

I hold my breath deep inside and glance very quickly behind me to make sure there's no one there but the darkness. Then I carefully bring myself over to the threshold and enlarge the crack enough to observe the unexpected gathering, my eyes on Hans, making sure not to push back the tapestry too much.

"Can I offer you a drink? Beer?"

"Well, sure, I'll have a cold one." Hans disappears into the kitchen and I hear the heavy breath of his sister's husband: "Indeed, indeed," he says half-aloud, and at the same time he appears vividly to me on the other side of the covering; I see all his gestures, the smallest movements and the facial expressions. I can even see how he's dressed.

After a fair while, a bit longer than it takes one to get two beers out of a fridge, Hans walks back into frame and puts the cans on the table. He straightens, stands motionless, looks straight ahead. At something that seems to make him happy, though his smile is rather more disapproving than warm. Has the visitor fallen asleep? I ask myself and watch Hans wipe his hand over his face, plunk himself down on the couch and sit back. Plunk himself? No, Hans does not really plunk. He just sits on the couch and leans slowly back. He seems tired. My delicate genius. How I long to crawl through the crack and into his lap, to tell him I just had to get inside the dark for a while until my painkiller kicked in. But I don't do that because I fear he would ask why I didn't just get under the blanket as usual. I'm afraid he'll go to see what's hidden behind the door, that it might be something other than I've surmised. More than anything, I am afraid he'll just take me in his arms and not ask a thing.

Hans reaches for his beer, takes a sip and looks at the clock. He stands back up. When I hear that he has shut himself inside the bathroom, I push the door carefully open and stick my head out. I get up, close it, and speed past the open-mouthed, snoring seminar participant.

When I get into the corridor, I let myself consider throwing on a jacket and acting as though I'd just popped out, but by now Hans is opening the bathroom door so I have no option other than the nearest door to me. It's the door to the basement and before I know it I'm in the storage area. From there, unfortunately, there's no way out of the house.

What's my story here? What is it that it has taken me about half an hour to find, which is how much time I estimate has passed since Hans returned home? I look over a stack of cardboard boxes standing on the floor up against the wall by the door. I find a box of photographs. Of course! I'm looking for an old photo! But I do not have much time so, without thinking about it, I take the one that's top of the pile. And I almost run up the stairs and into the apartment.

We meet in the middle of the hallway. I extend the photo in a rather agitated way and precipitously inform Hans that Mom wants to make a copy of this picture and frame it for herself. He does not say anything. Just looks at me somewhat oddly. It's what the photo shows: my parents up against a stone wall in the back garden with my grandmother, sometime in the early 1970s. Or, rather the fact that the photo I have in my hand is an inferior version of a picture already in my parents' home. In a frame with other family photos on the desk inside my father's office. Or does he look questioningly at me because I have suddenly appeared here from the basement with an old photo, wearing a nightdress, about half an hour after he's come home from work? For one moment, I hope that he will get his bearings, come over to me, that we'll look each other in the eye and know my conduct is no coincidence, which will give me the opportunity to tell him everything, of the great misfortune that befell me about a month ago. But just when I feel that Hans is about to open his mouth, a noise can be heard from inside the living room. His sister's husband has leapt up from his alcoholic doze, knocking over the glass vase that stood on the table next to the sofa. Passivity seals our fate, and soon we're both standing in the living room. The leather-vested political scientist in front of us is apologizing in a flurry, then suddenly, cheerfully cursing as he drops to the floor and starts picking up glass fragments, finding himself unable to work out what to do with them. He seems to have forgotten Hans saying he did not know where I was because he doesn't seem surprised to see me appear in the living room in my nightdress so late in the afternoon, standing there giving him amiable instructions about leaving things alone, don't worry about any of this.

As I sweep up the fragments, the brothers-in-law walk to the front door. They're talking, but I can't hear them. I take the dustpan out of the living room, but instead of heading right to the kitchen, my way leads into the bathroom where I thrust my face into the toilet bowl. And while I throw up, I go back over the images in the gold frame, the silent communication between the woman and the man in tweed that ended with him crawling out of the frame on all fours. The woman's face which I never saw. According to medical science, a meaningless, inexplicable image composed from the material that sends messages between our cells. A picture created from a disturbance that gives rise to a hammering blow inside my head. But if its source wasn't my own experience, where did it come from? Wasn't it I who called it forth? I deliberate whether the picture could be a scene from a movie or a novel I'd read and which had developed in my head in a slightly altered, distorted way, dissimilar enough that I did not understand the connection. Then I remembered the newspaper. Something tells me I've seen that front page and its photograph before. Is it even possible to make up images without a template?

I stand in front of the sink, turn on the water, and lean down to the faucet to get a mouthful. I look up and see Hans standing behind me. He walks in, embraces me around my sore waist. He puts his face against my throat and kisses me, looking directly into the mirror as he smiles: "Aren't you happy with the new curtains?"

I have to admit that I don't entirely understand where Mom is headed with these words. I'm not sure she knows, either

It was not until I got into bed last night that I thought about the notebook. As I watched from behind the door, Mom seemed to have just set it on the pile of books on the table. I have no way of telling if she opened it or not, but the sort of person who uses a key to get into someone else's home and hang curtains for them is hardly averse to snooping inside something like a little pink book. And that would mean she knows her shame as she stands here at my dining table working hard to adjust the tray of canapé pastries she has arranged for the social gathering that's about to begin.

But what is there to celebrate? Does anyone know? The new curtains? No, this is a banquet my mother was already planning just before we returned home. Probably in order to give the signal that my homecoming meant nothing, was just an intermediate moment, a turning point in the process, even if not all the pieces were in place. But even that occasion is a lost cause, ultimately undermined, because "my people," to quote Ester, have been constantly knocking on our door, ever since we moved in. And so there's no reunion needed, as was originally the plan.

I look at my guests chatting together. Mom's guests. Their gestures and expressions. Everything indicates without a doubt that
these dissimilar people, "my people," have found their so-called
common ground. But, for sure, it's an empty deception. Everyone who has ever networked at a gathering knows that. From the
host's viewpoint as she monitors silent conversations and people's
gestures, it's easy to forget your own experiences as a guest and to
rejoice in the image apparent before you.

I stand with a bottle of wine in my hand and turn in a circle.
Take in the excellent atmosphere. Gréta standing by the bookcase
in a long wine-red leather jacket, holding her glass of white wine,
laughing with Bonný and Guðbjörg, who seem to be saying something together, half-laughing themselves, nodding their heads in
time as Gréta starts talking, offering a more serious interpretation
of their rather comic story. From the host's perspective, there's a
nice rhythm to it.

And slightly different from the rhythm in front of *The Three
Fates*. Some conflict is underway, albeit a minor one, one quite
appropriate to a group of people getting together. The woman is
talking about some local politics, as I hear when I fill her interlocutor's red wine glass. He stands in his socks, wearing over a
beige khaki shirt a knit vest buttoned up to his neck, looking
down into his freshly filled glass, nodding his head, then shaking his head with jerky movements back and forth in courteous
protest; as the woman holds her hand aloft to put her case more
forcefully, the young man leans back all the way against the tapestry, so that the door handle touches his back. As far as I can see.
He looks upward to gather strength for his response. An answer
he ought to be well able to give being an expert on the subject.

That's why I have no reason to believe that this conversation between Bjarnfríður Una and Hans's brother-in-law is some kind of a game. Their gestures seem genuine. Their communications are, therefore, an exception to the rules about the host's willing deception.

But could such deception also cover the exchange of words between a younger woman and older man who have found a place at this very moment in the dining room? How sincere is my father's interest in Tína's speech as she flicks her long hair, underscoring her words with her delicate hands? I ask because Dad is strangely motionless in front of her. Entirely rigid. Shouldn't he move about a bit, show some kind of expression, anything? Perhaps he is so busy listening to the young actress that he does not need to pretend with his body the way you do when you have lost your interlocutor's thread at a party. Or so I think as I go into the kitchen to fetch yet another bottle of wine.

When I return to the dining room, Tína's disappeared. Dad is standing alone with his wine glass, smiling over the room, still happy as Sigga D. walks across to him. He sets down the glass and takes a tight hold of my childhood friend. Their vignette begins with a question and quick reply and continues on as I watch or until I look out over another corner of the living room. Ester and the teenager, Hans's niece, are there. They aren't talking. Why are they standing there? Had they been talking and just now stopped? Did Ester bring up something that this chip off her father's shoulder didn't want to be party to? What would be her mother's take, my sister-in-law? That her daughter does not care for small talk. What can the science of mindfulness teach us about these circumstances? And where is my sister-in-law leading my mother with her words? Mom is staring down at the floor, probably to give the impression of unusually focused attention and interest in what my sister-in-law is trying to explain. Here's another kind of exception: in this case I, the host, do not accept the deception; Mom has no appetite for what my sister-in-law has to share, so she lowers her head and takes the time to consider the lecturer's footwear. And here I butt in, for their glasses are empty, catching the final words of this Puss in Boots: "to be the director of your own life," at which Mom places her glass under the bottle mouth and praises me for her own food and drink, letting hang in the air the mismatched metaphor, these lofty words of wisdom my sister-in-law had offered as a way to fix the mess our lives had become.

And the wisdom persists until my father-in-law walks onto the stage. He greets my mother with the pretense of respect and strange formalities. The sister-in-law, however, lets herself vanish, popping up next between her daughter and Ester, seemingly having contrived to build some bridge. My sister-in-law is very much at home in Ester's world, and, although this world may not be an adolescent one, the teenager is her mother's daughter, and they seem in concert, even though they are little alike. For, despite all the talk, this generation of children is usually closely connected to their parents who, denying their own age, have become part of the life and culture of their offspring.

I clink glasses with my father-in-law, and when he has thanked me, he begins to ask Mom about the exhibition of the young artist, the mirror woman, which opened in the Art Museum a few days back. "You see, I have to confess that I don't entirely understand the idea behind the work." I don't care one bit to take a stance against my father-in-law's words, and even less to listen to a well-phrased, learned reply from Mom, but her set expression puts me in a difficult spot: she looks thoughtfully at her conversation partner, my father-in-law, squinting, as one might, but then she also looks right ahead at me so that I'm stuck fast; she freezes me inside the picture before she makes her speech:

"Listen. The viewer only sees the work from one angle at a time. But by moving about, he comes to sees how the face of one historical figure transforms into an image of another famous person from the past, except one of a different gender. And as you've no doubt seen for yourself, there is no coincidence who transforms into whom." Then she glances up, adjusts her hair, and continues to talk about how these dual portraits shake up the conventional wisdom that history is a story spun by powerful, victorious forces; she talks about the many threads that inhere in the past, the one reliable knowledge history can bring us: "I should say that the past literally rises up through this work. Rises up and places itself in sight of the viewer, reminding him how she is more or less a product of his perspective."

Renaissance man, dressed in a polo sweater, whose color I do not entirely trust myself to accurately describe in words, and a thin wool jacket with some tiny insignia high up on the collar, looks down. I look at his face, how he pauses and pouts his wet lips. Should I take my chance to disappear? But then, without meeting my eyes, he takes my shoulder, indicating that I'm not going anywhere. At the same time, it becomes clear to me that he's given up on reacting to Mom's verbal torrent, that he's using me to change the topic: "But *you*, on the other hand, are doing something remarkable, I'm told! Have managed to find *their* first female painter, those Englishmen!" He smiles gently and asks: "But does that change our perception and understanding of the artist's work, his position within art history?"

Sometimes I have found that my insecurity toward other people is in opposition to my respect for them: the less I respect someone, the more insecure I will be toward them. But that's not the only reason I can't come up with any words for my father-in-law at this moment; in my head there are no answers to such questions. But Mom is still here. How very fortunate:

"Of course that changes things in a historical sense, no need to even waste words on that! But more than that, when we're talking about a relatively unknown artist from such a remote period of history, their gender may also have a different significance. You see, in today's historiography, where the focus on the individual is once again becoming stronger, it's actually better for a forgotten artist to have been a woman than a man. What used to work against the artist has become her success."

I have to admit that I don't entirely understand where Mom is going with these words. I'm not sure she knows, either, but she's clearly going somewhere. She puts her hands in her pants pockets, bounces on her toes, and heads off. But my father-in-law does not see that at first, so absorbed is he in his skepticism and Mom's words; before he can gainsay them, I lift the wine bottle in the air, unnecessarily high, as if to suggest there must be guests around with empty glasses. And with that I budge slowly away from my father-in-law, the art-inclined, culturally-minded empiricist.

Mom has installed herself with Dad and Sigga D. I see the three talking as I enter the kitchen to get one more bottle. They are merry until Sigga starts shaking her head between them as she looks in my direction, inquiringly. I pour some wine into my glass, although I know I must not drink a drop while taking my medicine. I look at my parents. Sigga has gone. Dad looks at

Mom. I look at him looking at her, how his face is dissolving and running together with the hazy environment of the living room. Until everything is a fog, although Mom's image is sharpening, moving somehow beyond the three-dimensional, blurred background. She's wearing a black wool jacket over a tightly-woven shirt, white and collarless. There is nothing to disturb that picture except perhaps the slim gold band on her ring finger when she strokes her silver-gray bob to pat down anything that might have gone haywire, though nothing, of course, has. I steady myself against the kitchen sink, I'm losing my balance. The living room is ebbing away, but the image of Mom has become more focused, higher in the air than ever before, she somehow doesn't seem a part of this environment. But when I head in her direction, something black appears in front of her. Something on her shirt. First, it seems like letters. RC and maybe A. But then the letters start to move and become a pattern that reminds me instead of a coat of arms. I reach my hand out to stop myself falling.

He lay on his side in his suit the
way he would at a picnic, though I'd
never seen him lying like that on
the living room floor before

I wake myself up by knocking one hand against the bedside table lamp. In my dream, I'd wanted my notebook, which was lying on the nightstand. As soon as I open my eyes I know why. There's an image in my head, and I must write it down before it disappears. I reach for a pen, which is on the windowsill and which I don't recognize having seen before. One of Hans's writing implements, a little peculiar, probably from the laboratory. I open the book to the back because the image in my head is really beyond its contents. But just as I mean to start writing, something quite strange happens. Instead of fading away slowly and surely, as dream visions are meant to, the image in my head becomes ever clearer, and the clearer it becomes the more difficulty I have finding the words to describe it. Without thinking, I start drawing in the book, and then it's almost like I'm stroking across the page in soft strips with thick ink. Like the model is lying underneath the paper. Hair frames the woman's face, a forelock falling over one eye beside a round-tipped nose. I cut the picture off at the woman's chest and outstretched arms; in her raised palm sits a tiny little girl. And now I can see who it is. I see what this is. This is the picture that appeared to me just before I fell to the floor at the gathering yesterday evening. A picture of Mom as she stepped forward like some giant to seize me with both hands while my guests stared at me, petrified. Not displaying any reaction other than expressions that said, "What misfortune is this?" What happened next can, however, be explained only in words. I write immediately. Right below the picture. And then over to the next open page.

I close the notebook and set it on the bedside table. Lie on my pillow and look, lost in thought, at the ceiling rosette above me. Then I roll onto my side and watch the cover lift slowly from the pages. I reach into the book and open it to the front: the text about *the Demolitionist*. For the meeting with Diana that never came to pass.

"Everything looks better on paper"? What had Diana and my sister-in-law's guru meant by these words? This writing of mine about the demolitionist does not look at all good on paper, nor did these reflections of mine, laid bare on paper, reveal their "petty, impetuous" nature. In other words, I would have to admit to everything stated there, but like much of what one thinks about, I only wanted to keep the reflections for myself.

I look at the spine and see that the paper has not been cut in a way that the pages could easily tear out. I'll need to get them out some other way. Throw them into the trash, I think, and head to do it.

I walk into the living room and from there into the dining room. Glasses and dishes all over the place. Someone has washed up and arranged things neatly on the table. But where is Hans?

Gone to work so early on a Saturday morning? I put the notebook in the breast pocket of my nightshirt, put my hands on the table edge and lean forward. The image that appeared to me in the living room for just a moment is right now being called up in my mind. I can't bring myself to look back, at my tapestry, which now lies crumpled on top of the books in front of the door. The door is open, but only a slit. Had Bjarnfríður Una and Hans's sister's husband talked about regional affairs? Here? He had leaned against the hanging so the handle touched his back. Leaned his head back and looked at the ceiling in a concentrated search for the right words for the obvious. Did they know one another from up north?

I turn around and move myself closer. I grasp the handle and open the door wider. I step up to the threshold and stick my head in. The material caresses my face. I open the door wide. Across the opening there's a clothesline from which hang three white smocks. Doctor's coats. A fourth is on the floor. I push the gowns away with a gentle but firm movement. I'm startled by my own scream, surging up powerfully, like thunder, but soon find myself emitting a miserable whine as I make out who stands there before me. The face is snowy white but the eyes are fixed, circled in a black ring of old eye-shadow. The remnants of red color on my dried-out lips. I quickly glance away from my own reflection, look down at the floor, at the three walls. Then back up to the frame around a mirror, at a small card that has been tucked in its lower right corner: *Dr. Theodor Jakobsson, M. D. Tel. 2319.*

The wide expanse within me. Nothing but a clothes closet, no more than a meter square! I pick the gown up off the floor, stroke the white linen, and bring it up to my face before I cast it back down on the floor. I'm filled with a strange emptiness, unable to tell whether it's anything but a search for something that's not nearly as vast as it once seemed. A space that is no longer there when looked at more closely. I lean up against the door frame and allow myself to slide down to the floor. I don't imagine I will get back up anytime soon.

I let my eyes fix on the darkness in the left-hand corner of the closet, on some card lying there. Did it fall from the pocket of the doctor's smock? I stare without seeing. Perhaps I've had enough of my own perception for a while. I lie for a long time thinking very little, nothing more than about the colors I think I can make out on the card, how they little by little brighten the longer I stare. At one point, I think there's a very small light shining in the corner. Now I come to see it must be a postcard. I lie halfway across the floor and reach out for it.

La muse. The very small woman who encountered me here in the closet a few days ago? I turn the card over. It's addressed to Dr. and Mrs. Theodor. The writing is minute. It has to be some of the smallest writing I'd ever seen:

London, August 30, 1960

Dear ma and dear pa!
I simply must share from afar that A. passed the exam with flying colors and has been accepted into the school. What a joy! We now have a few days to enjoy life here in the city. Today we visited the Tate Gallery, Britain's national art museum. We had to wait in line outside the museum for a whole two hours in scorching heat, would you believe it, because there's an on-going exhibition of the celebrated Picasso's work (see picture on the

back)—*remember, Dad, you showed me a review of the exhibi-*
tion in the paper just before we left. Here, as a matter of fact,
everyone is going crazy for some reason, talking about a veri-
table Picassomania in this country, even though avant-garde
art has been very much in the bad books here. The Queen's
husband made it clear that the painter was clearly a drunk,
must be, given his politics and support for communism. But the
Queen and her mother were moved and found themselves more
than a little intoxicated looking at man's inner face of man,
visible in the painter's distorted visages.

Your little,

H

Up against the left edge of the postcard, actually on top of the
writing itself, was written: *p.s. I do not know if the honored couple*
back home on Túngata might be interested in this news!

I turn the card around. I sniff the image. The honored couple
on Túngata? H and A? Hrefna The and my mom? If my world
had collapsed on itself when I looked into the closet a moment
back, it now expanded out at terrible speed. Headed full force out
into the scattered expanses of childthought, without any perception of an ending, just the marvels of eternity in a child's tiny
world:

My earliest memory. The starting point of my life; under it,
the distant sound of singing. An old recording, which sounded
like butter spattering in a frying pan: "My friend Tito Schipa," as
grandfather referred to his favorite singer. Grandmother standing
at the dining table in her shining shirtwaist dress, putting things
into her handbag. I tried to get her attention with my words, but

when she did not answer me, I tugged at her dress. My grandmother swatted her hand behind her in my direction, driving
me back to my nook next to the big cupboard of books, locked
behind glass, where I continued my game, feeling the cold, cutting silence brush my back when she walked past me and out of
the room. Out of the house and probably down Túngata.

Now it was only grandfather and me. Looking under the
cupboard, I saw his foot, the patterned tips of his cognac-brown
brogues. The room thick with smoke from his big cigar. Grandfather had said something to grandmother that I had not heard
well, but just before she left the room, he said: "To pretend the
child has learning difficulties as a way to cover up her illness indicates a sick mindset." I did not understand what he meant, surely,
and I doubt, of course, as I recall his words, that I can in fact have
heard them right back then. Especially after having spent the next
few years forgetting them thanks to what happened next:

I carefully peeked my face out past the book cupboard; at that
same moment, my grandfather looked up from his newspaper.
The paper cut off his face just below the eyes, his attentive glance
right above the photo on the cover showing Mom, a pinhead in
the midst of the thousands of people who had gathered around
the unremarkable clock to mark the day's famous occasion: The
1975 Women's Day Off. About this event, my grandmother and
Mom had talked with some hostility the day before. Continuing
it, Grandmother and Grandfather's silent warfare reached their
high-mark the next day. The day it became clear the event was
unique, probably historic. The day grandfather's eyes met mine.
The day he came crawling on all fours over to my corner, getting
incredibly excited about my toy: his leather-covered pen box, silk
needle cushion and a golden thimble from Grandmother's sewing

chest. A gridded teak trivet for hot pans. He lay on his side in his suit the way he would at a picnic, though I'd never seen him lying like that on the living room floor before. Once Grandfather had let Barbie sit on the pin cushion and drink from the thimble, he put the doll down for a nap on the pen case behind the partition, the teak trivet. Then he, too, went to sleep. He fell to his side and straight onto his stomach. And there he lay while I played. Right up until Grandmother returned.

She appears in the door. Suddenly, as quietly as she'd disappeared earlier that day. But she's a different grandmother. With her handbag on her slender arm, she puts both hands around her head, shaking it unceasingly. Emaciated, almost deformed, her face seems to indicate she's screaming, but I can't hear a thing. She walks toward Grandfather, slips her handbag off her shoulder, and lets it fall to the floor beside him. She grasps his shoulder, rolls him on his back and begins to shake him and slap his face. She looks around like a frightened animal in search of an escape route. And it was then that she realizes that I was standing there in the living room, had fled over to the corner as she came in, my back straight as a rod, hands reaching down my sides to my flame-red overalls, trying to figure out whether I am more terrified or surprised. Grandma gets up, reaches out her hand and walks slowly toward me. Puts one hand over my eyes, the other on my neck. I stand deathly still, but when I feel almost out of breath, I try to take her hands from my face. Then she grasps me in her arms, and holds me tightly, so my first reaction is to free myself. I push with both hands against her thin shoulders, my little paws on the sheer, shining fabric of her paisley shirtwaist dress. She resists me, clutches one hand around my neck and presses my face into her collarbone. Then I feel myself stiffen, stubborn as anything, responding with some deep and terrible strength, putting both hands on her face to get rid of her. A face I realize I've never touched before. I push my fingers up into her skin, drag them along her cheekbone until her soft, elastic skin almost lies across her eye. The image I see brings a scream forth from somewhere inside me, and with it a surge of strength that ends with me on the floor, flat on my stomach, like Grandfather, until my grandmother's thin hands clasp around my waist and try to pull me back to her. But then her grip is suddenly released; at that same moment, I am taken hold of firmly under my arms, and jerked up. In the dark under my eyelids, I recognize Daddy's stubble as it tickles my nose, the smell of his skin calming this child's overstretched nerves. In the distance, I hear a peculiar sound from my grandmother and Mom and then two loud male voices alternately giving orders, and Grandfather is carried out.

I don't remember if I got any help to forget about this experience, or whether I did forget about it at all, because the event and grandfather's last words became a sort of black hole for everything related to my young mother, her education and possible illnesses. The first lines in my image of Mom were likely drawn right there.

I get up from the floor and go into the kitchen. In the earthenware bowl on top of the fridge I find the photo of my parents. A photograph that I had used two days ago as a sort of absenteeism for being inside a concrete-walled clothes closet! Dad is standing on the left with a sweater around his shoulders, somehow timeless compared to the classic 1960s image beside him: my mom's hair is thick, cut short, straightened. She wears a man's short-sleeved shirt over tight-fitting pants, pants secured with a wide belt around her slender waist. Mom has one foot on a rock wall, narrow-toed flat. Around her neck a bandana, half-hidden behind the smoke entering into the frame from the right, from the cigarette that someone beside her has pinched between an index and middle finger.

But this photo was not taken in the backyard of my mother's childhood home, as I've always imagined. I can see that now. I can see it in my mother's face. The picture wasn't even taken in Iceland. This is not an Icelandic rock Mom's leaning on, resting her foot against. It's brick. English brick. London in the fall of 1960? Dad adjusts the sweater on his shoulders before he walks out of the picture. Mom follows him. To Iceland, at grandmother's request. Away from Sixties Britain, that great beginning of history. Toward her destiny as an Icelandic housewife, my dad's wife and, after a painful ordeal, my mother.

I look at the piled, stony wall in the picture, and feel like it's going to break apart and fall on top of me. Countless images arrange themselves above one another, voices talking on top of each other. Then silence rings out. It's the silence under Mom's words from last night: You see, in today's historiography, where the focus on the individual is once again becoming stronger, it's actually better for a forgotten artist to have been a woman than a man. What used to work against the artist has become her success."

What had sounded simply like erudite chatter directed at my father-in-law's ears during yesterday evening's festivities was clearly a message. A message to me. Mom had worked out my problem. Either when she went through *Sex, Gender,* etc. here in the living room two days ago, or yesterday when she checked out my notebook while I was hiding in the closet. At least, she had put two and two together and was now telling me to stick to my course. But her declaration of support, her promise of concealment, had been disguised. She knew I would never ask her to keep secret such a serious act, so she was having to pretend I don't know she knows what has happened. What I've done. Firmly resolved to make sure I don't lack what she lacked under grandmother's awful power, Mom has set her blessing on the deed; as amazing as it sounds, it's all I need to keep going. But to be absolutely sure about my understanding, I need to get some sign from her. I have to ask her a question. Face to face. Only one simple question and if she answers yes, I will go ahead and submit my thesis.

I've swept my hair into a pony tail and come into the front room. I button myself up and step into my shoes with the gold buckles on the instep. I tie the belt of my overcoat and my footsteps click smartly on the entryway floor as I reach for the knob. Like someone accepting a command from on high.

I'm standing on the threshold. The cold breeze strokes my face from the right as it moves west. It's rather ominous. But I will not let that stop me. My journey to Mom will not take more than fifteen minutes or so. Am I forgetting something?

To my mother

The houses here farthest up the street are stone, mostly painted white; lower down they're identical constructions, yet multi-colored. A Reykjavík street scene with a hazy, fragmented history.

I've just gone down the stairs and out onto the sidewalk as a fancy automobile, a Lexus, drives past the house. Far above the speed limit. I watch the car. Was that the Reverend Sigurður? Gotten so thin-haired in these twenty years that have passed since he floated, white-clad and tanned, across the flashing dance-floor toward me. Waving his hands, shaking his pretty hips, so that I dared not answer any other way than to adjust my shoulder pads in time with my automatic foot movements. That evening had started at Sigga D.'s home, but I was now all alone inside the venue because she had been stopped at the entrance for being underage. Instead of turning back and going out with her, I'd moved on into the dark cave, on toward the dance floor. Not yet come of age, a sweatband around my forehead, on a victory high, without a way to communicate it except for these awkward, cun-ningly-conceived movements in front of this breathtaking young guy. I don't remember how long the dance lasted, but I remember too well how the evening ended. I stood by the cloakroom, leaning my back up against the rough, dark-colored wall. All around me things were taking shape, but I was not part of any of these intrigues, even though I made it look like I was looking for some imaginary companions there amid the throng. Forlorn, suddenly so young and alone that I couldn't find a way to either stay put or walk on out. Then he appeared all at once from the hall, grinning broadly and dripping with sweat after his exertions. Streams of bliss surged through my body, and I got busy adjusting the wide belt around my waist. But when I stole a look, I realized his smile wasn't for me, but for two women his own age standing right in front of me. Just before the three of them left the place, dashing and caught up in some kind of dance, he looked toward me. But his smile contained no brightness; instead, everything had darkened, and I felt my life would come to an end there in the cloakroom queue. There was this relaxed quality to the smile that turned his greeting into a symbol for all of life's incomprehensible, merciless moments from that point on. Or at least until I saw him long after that, presiding at the altar, ordaining them in marriage: Guðbjörg, today a realtor, and the man whose name I no longer remember. A marriage that was no more successful than the awkward metaphors this former king of the dance floor offered the bridal couple, ramblings about "love and life." As I sat at the front of the church that day, I recalled my mother's reaction when I had returned home from the discotheque some fifteen years earlier, cold and swollen with tears, having walked through town. If only I had understood her words and wisdom back then.

As I approach the first intersection, I see a young man coming out of the supermarket on the corner at a run. He's holding a plastic bag and heads toward a car that has been parked up on the sidewalk of the street opposite. Just before the man disappears into the car, he moves his hand in my direction, but I cannot answer his greeting because my first reaction is to look down at the sidewalk, and when I look back he's vanished inside his car. When the car has reached the next street corner, I realize who it was. And at the same time, I know why I looked down and away. The young man in the car is a composer. He is married to one of Tína's friends.

A dinner party. Approximately five years ago. I hear words rush out into the air. Words about music. Highfalutin, intoxicated words about music, the obtrusive words of a layman in search of a specialist's recognition, the person sitting next me. Had he listened to me out of interest or pity? I was never sure, not for weeks buried under replays of this asinine scene in my head, but now his weightless wave and the smile accompanying it confirm the latter; in his smirk, there's no doubting the message, that despite such a long time having passed, my musical idiocies could still be made fun of. But as soon as I understand that, I also know nothing can alter the fact that my logic that evening is his lone source of knowledge about me. My words are tantamount to *who I am* in his eyes and the eyes of all those he might have shared my drivel with. If, that is, I've ever gotten a mention among his crowd.

I'm wondering how likely that is when I hear a car horn. I've half-crossed the road, and the car is almost upon me. The man behind the wheel lifts his hand questioningly in the air. I retreat and step back up onto the sidewalk. The car drives on and the woman in the passenger seat shoots me a searching glance. An overly intense reaction, given the situation, I think to myself, but before I can follow that thought to its end, her face reappears in my memory. From a short time before Hans and I moved away. She's standing at a table inside a large hall at a suburban charity fundraiser. On the table there's red fabric, a thin, crushed velvet, material for a party dress being used as a tablecloth. I'm on a girls' night out with Sigga D., at Bjarnfríður Una's invitation. The lady from the passenger seat had turned to me to talk about international aid organizations. Inviting me to sponsor a child, to become a so-called "Global" parent. Because I did not know what sum of money was involved, I suspected the requisite generosity was beyond me, so I replied with considerable agitation, lying that I was already a "Global" parent, then walked away in the direction of the table where the winetasting was taking place. And as I stood there, a glass in one hand and morsels of cheese in the other, I watched Sigga fill out a piece of paper this same woman had handed her, as Bjarnfríður stood by and nodded helpfully. Like someone who knows from experience. Bjarnfríður the global mother to many children? But how in heaven's name had I thought up this excuse? It's not like lying to a youngster in the lobby of a mall that you already bought a little furry creature to support a charity for alcoholics earlier that day. In some other store.

I've crossed the street and am standing before a big white stone house. One that stands so much more prominently than any of the others. I slow down and look at the elegant entryway, the steps up to the massive front door, look in the living room window, at the white, silk-smooth replicas of *Boy and Girl* and of *The Water Carrier*. An older man emerges from the house and says hello to me as I stand by the garden side. He does so only out of politeness, I doubt he remembers me. Not the way I remember him, through tears that little by little blurred my vision of his face.

A white medical gown that blended with the wall behind him as I made a cellphone call to the indifferent Hans, who at the time was only two kilometers away from me, in the large conference hall, a glass of wine in his hand, together with his Icelandic colleagues, while on the right huddled clusters of molecular biologists, small groups orbiting the same nucleus. When had the guy received the Nobel Prize? Had Hans ever gotten to talk to him? Had it been my very phone call that ended that tremendous opportunity for my loving sweetheart, my words spoken in a cracking voice, telling him how our little thing had come to nothing, that he needed to come right away? When he asked me if I couldn't take a cab home from the hospital, my pain altered into the peculiar well-being necessitated by sudden revulsion toward one's loved ones. No, I no longer wanted anyone beside me, not even Daddy or Mom. I resolved to thrive on the pain, to walk on through this suffering alone.

I spent the next few days mostly with the comforter over my head, unable to bear how Hans's puppy eyes stared at me whenever I moved around our tiny student apartment. His facial expression, which meant to express regret, seemed to me nothing but an automatic request for immediate forgiveness so that we could go back to living our lives. A hasty absolution so that he could continue working toward his goal. He couldn't afford to lose any time.

When I am just a few steps past the doctor's beautiful white home, I hear in the distance a crying baby. A woman of my age, with short-cut dark hair, walks briskly toward me, hoping that the speed of the stroller she pushes away from herself will comfort the child lying inside. She does not look at me but I see her face clearly. See it even once she's passed me. She looks at me from twenty years ago. She is in horrendous shock. She's screaming, but I cannot hear anything because of the loud music carrying from somewhere, some nearby neighborhood in a foreign city. All there is is her long, dark hair swinging back and forth almost in line with her body which hangs in the open air, hands on the balcony rail. I bring myself over to the railing and take her arms, but swiftly realize this won't work. I'll never be able to lift her up. I'm trying to call for help but no words come because it's so far down and I'm dizzy and I have to let go of her slender wrists to steady myself and take a step back onto the tiled balcony floor. A mosque and a few spires reflect the burning sun, half gone behind the horizon. Who is that snaking through the picture like lightning? The Queen of Sheba, King Solomon! Get me away from here!

And then finally things opened up and I was able to call for help. But at the same moment, I fall to the balcony floor under a blow from someone who comes running out onto the balcony and pushes me down, allowing the upper part of their body to lean out over the balcony, to grab the girl's waist and pull her to one side and up with heavy pants, and then the girl is throwing one foot over the railing and helping out with her own rescue. The girl lands on the floor but stands up right away, pushing herself away from the young man who now came running out onto the balcony; she goes crying into the hotel room. Bjarnfríður Una plunks herself down with her back to the balcony railing and hand over her mouth. She does not look at me. She looks straight ahead and is close to petrified. I stand by her side and look down at the tiles. I listen to the voice shout inside me and feel for a moment that my next step can only be replaying again the recklessness of our school friend, a girl we didn't know well but who we'd still followed from the farewell party of our graduation trip abroad to a hotel room, where we tried in vain to reassure her after her ferocious argument with her boyfriend. I take hold of the railing and lean my head down and torment my cowardly soul by staring seven stories below to the street. When I look up, the sun has set and the music gone quiet, though from inside the room carry choked sobs and, mixed with them, low whispering. Bjarnfríður has gone back in and is standing in front of the couple, nodding hesitantly at their wish that "this," as the young man calls the incident, not go any further.

We leave the room and head down to another floor. Bjarnfríður worried, doubtful about the promise we had ended up giving, acting like I don't exist. I scream silently, alone inside myself.

I look at the clock. I'm about halfway through my journey to Mom, and I walk faster as I feel raindrops on one of my cheeks. From my raincoat pocket sounds a tinny noise, quiet to begin with but getting gradually louder. Sigga D. thanks me for last night and asks how I'm doing. However, she does not mention a word about how last night's gathering possibly, most likely, ended. She talks, on the other hand, about chatting with my parents, says how nice it was to see them. Then she says something I do not hear well because of the traffic. "Hold on," I say, and step into a narrow passageway between two houses. I stand at the far end of the passageway, which looks into a remote backyard, and give Sigga a signal to continue. "I was asking why you're always telling people I don't like my job? Your mom asked me last night, not for the first time, when I was finally going to follow my dream and go back to school. For literature!"

I look up into the black sky, past the alien backsides of houses I never knew existed. At a slender, short woman who walks out onto one of the balconies. The woman lights a cigarette and I say something to Sigga about how I feel she never talks about her work, so much less than the fiction she's reading. "Which *you* are reading," she says, "And why, do you think?" I say I can't answer that, I'm in a hurry. I need to say goodbye to her.

The woman on the balcony, who seems middle-aged, leans over the railing as a teenage boy appears behind her and starts to tug at her sweater. Because of his size and build, I guess he wants her to come in and get him something to eat. From the food filling all the cupboards and cabinets hidden inside the kitchen of this residence, which hides itself away behind the visible street scene. How would you get inside this house? Through this passageway? Past three words that have been scrawled so crudely here on the wall and which I notice on my way back to the main road? I realize how repugnant they are as soon as it dawns on me that I am not getting out of the passageway any time soon: rainwater forms a tight wall in front of me. The black cloud. I decide to use the time to call Sigga back. To greet her more kindly, with excuses and promises to contact her later today. I take the phone out of my coat pocket and look at the screen. Twenty new messages. A week old, all from Bonný. I know it will take a while before I go over them all, but the beginning of the first message is enough to make me wait to call Sigga: *You are missing a lot, hon!* I glance through the disjointed texts. There's a whole mass. I lean against the graffitied wall, against that dirty Icelandic word I've never been able to put in my mouth. Support myself on it as I patch the fragments from Bonný together into my mind and fill in the story by dint of what I know. And some imagination:

They'd arrived at the cottage about five-ish. Sigga immediately turned on the water and gas; some of them went out on the deck and praised the view and talked about how long it had been since they last were there, but Bjarnfríður Una had no sooner slipped off her shoes than she was arranging snacks and cheese on a tray which she laid on the new coffee table. In fact, she'd pushed the table top to the side before laying the tray on it to see if there was something newer in the cabinet under the panel than the years-old *Weekly News* from their last visit (I just know she did).

Shortly after that, the cooking began. Bjarnfríður opened the first red wine bottle of many that she set out as part of her generous contribution to the celebration. It was a fine French wine that she had bought wholesale through her acquaintances. The group was relaxed and there was much merriment over the table. Some rapid drinking. Ester most of all, and by the time coffee was served she had suddenly begun to talk, out of thin air, about sex. And not just sex in general. She talked about the married couple's sex life. In their row house. The forest green one. In the suburbs. Sigga A. got up quickly and went to sleep. She had, as usual, been silent, but this time for a reason Sigga D. will tell me about later, Bonný writes. But to clear the air after Ester's frankness, because all of her sex talk had a very positive note, which made it even more unbearable than otherwise, Sigga, the heir to the cabin, suggested they move over to the sofa and play a game of trivia. The idea was met with appreciation.

Glasses were moved between tables while Sigga fetched the game. Everything went well, and the women's "ignorance" brought forth old memories and laughter. But when the game was about half over, the competition took an unexpected turn, beginning with Tína's question for Bjarnfríður Una: "What French writer is the author of these words: *Everything leads us to believe that there exists a spot in the mind where the real and the imaginary will cease to appear contradictory?"*

Tína looked at the answer, nodded to herself, of course, at the benefit of having the information on the card. She put it back in the deck, obviously not expecting much from Bjarnfríður's response; the latter squinted her eyes and stroked her lips.

Bjarnfríður racked her brain for a few seconds, then said, with some hesitation, and in fact, as a question: "André Breton himself, is it not?"

The whole group was silent. Tína looked questioningly into the eyes of her friend. Then she said, without hesitation: "André Breton himself? Is he a family member? You cheated!"

Bjarnfríður then turned big, questioning eyes on Tína: "Wait, how could I?"

"You peeked, or else you saw the answer earlier when you pulled two cards out of the box or something," answered Tína.

"I peeked," Bjarnfríður said, breathing deeply, "And who am I? Who am I, Tína? Who am I in your eyes?" She asked, her voice cracking. She leant half across the table to wait for Tína's response, as she sat there on the other side of it, looking upward as if to escape this question, which was about to blow up the paneled little cabin in West Iceland.

Bjarnfríður Una sat back on the couch and sipped her beer, swallowing a tidy burp and looking down. None of the women said a word. It's as though the atmosphere Bjarnfríður's existential question created weighed heavier than what Ester had conjured by sharing the secrets of her bedroom and the thickset ballplayer earlier this evening. It was so unbearable that not even Sigga D. could defuse it.

But now, just when you would think that the country cabin story is about to reach some sort of peak, it's like Bonný's thumb dropped off with all the texting. Her truncated, disjointed messages nevertheless let me know that the wretched Bjarnfríður Una seemed to have broken the silence and answered her question herself: "A cultureless, self-obsessed nag from the North." She had leaned back and repeated her words, now in the form of a question that she answered by taking the silent group of girlfriends twenty years back in time. This wouldn't have been an unfamiliar journey, given how often Bjarnfríður tells and has told the story of her becoming part of this group.

The story Bonný refers to here, which I had in fact long forgotten, and now remember as I stand in this passageway, sheltered from the pouring rain, started up north, in the small town of Húsavík. Bjarnfríður had lived there with her single mother since she was a toddler, but the real stage for the story is Reykjavík High School where she got to know her girlfriends and then-classmates. At Húsavík, the loud-voiced and powerful Bjarnfríður earned a good reputation within the town's amateur theater, and it was therefore natural that she joined the theater club at her new school when she came south. In the theater club, she soon met the big shot, a boy, a senior, who was fascinated with the self-certainty and talent of this rough-hewn northern belle. He never called her anything but Una.

But that fairytale did not last long. Tína, an elfish wanderer, suddenly got the acting bug too, and got caught up in the relationship between the promising young actor and Bjarnfríður. Caught up, in fact, in Bjarnfríður's chance of a dramatic career, because her position within the group diminished in the aftermath of all this, and she was eventually driven away. She was subsequently isolated from the girls who were her classmates, the girls who indirectly took up Tína's resentment because Bjarnfríður was a stranger from the north. One of us was the ringleader; Bonný, if I remember right. I don't quite know, however, whether it was Bjarnfríður's mother's illness or frustration with school that led to her decision to head back north to work in a fish-processing plant for the summer but the trip was still decisive because that autumn she returned south, sturdier than ever, her stocky prankster by her side. In fact, she herself had put on a little weight, too.

Gradually, Bjarnfríður started to hang around with this boy's friends, a right-wing group from the graduating class, more than her own peers. After all this fellowship had taken her in with open arms when Tína and her crowd betrayed her. And this signaled the marked start of a political identity for this young amateur actress from Húsavík, without there ever having been any kind of ideological revelation, nor was there any indication biology was a factor in her political orientation. Bjarnfríður Una simply did not think anything her saviors, the people right before her eyes, had to say about the role and purpose of contemporary politics could be anything but right and true.

Then a year later these two boyfriends, the actor and the conservative, disappeared from Bjarnfríður and Tína's lives. The classmates' friendship resumed, but without the former leaving her ex's social circle, those people who'd supported her so well. And so Bjarnfríður Una's position in life was fully established. Politics became her companionship, her refuge, rather than her passion and conviction. The same was true of Tína. She had gone onto the stage, where her interest in political theater was awakened, not necessarily due to her ideals but rather because it was her way to give her career as an actress more gravity when misgivings about the significance of the art began to occupy her mind. But that path—inevitably left-wing and radical—also signaled her ignorance of the more subtle texts in that genre and their impenetrable but powerful politics.

That's where my version of the story Bonný referenced ends. I look back down at the screen and the confusion of abbreviations displayed on it. It seemed that Tína had at the story's end moved over to her girlfriend, embracing her and saying that Bjarnfríður Una had a big heart, although she did not always speak like it. And that those who speak most loudly about compassion and the need for generosity in our world aren't always exemplary themselves. She knew that all too well; in reality, people were rarely in a position to show their true qualities; most of us never end up in such situations. Then she stood up and extended her delicate hand to her friend, the girlfriend whom she had indirectly, by stealing her boyfriend, pushed toward the very political associations she herself had spent her life condemning, and pulled her up from the couch: "And I've never said you were a cultureless hillbilly. Just never thought you were into French surrealism."

Bjarnfríður Una had put her hand to her chest and sat up with an innocent expression. They walked out onto the terrace. And that's how I see the story end before me: Tína putting a cigarette in her mouth, and then leaning down to Bjarnfríður's hand, which keeps the fire lit. They settle down on the wooden bench, feet crossed and up on the railing. In front of them the shrubs, the lake, the mountain and the sun behind them, silhouetted when seen from the living room, visibly sharing a sisterly cigarette in the evening quiet as the sun sinks down across the horizon.

It had stopped raining. A while ago. Why had Bonný sent me all this? I step out from the passageway, brush my hair off my face, tighten my ponytail and head down the street. Beyond all the cellar windows containing lives that seem cast aside, hidden behind strange trash on window ledges, behind curtains from another century, behind the panes' thick dust. I go past the house that was once a ship owner's wealthy estate but is now a guesthouse named, thanks to a homemade sign, after an Icelandic settler. Then I come to the end of the street and stand at Ragnar's Frameshop, which is in the house on the corner. I look into the store front, at a woman who stands beside a radiant, brand-new abstract painting, discussing the frame with a man behind the counter. Ragnar? I focus on the glass, pout my lips as soon as my reflection appears. I run my hands over my trench coat from the waist down and am about to turn up my collar when my focus expands to take in the store. On the wall above Ragnar hangs a big print, turbulent landscape in a golden frame. I get closer to the glass. The clouds fade and move slowly away. The colors dissolve into one another until my face lies superimposed on Turner's sky:

I look ahead. Which way should I go? Up these stairs? And into the building? Twenty-nine steps. I walk breathlessly through an opening between two columns and from there in through the tall door that stands open. Inside is an elegant hall and at the end of the hall are broad steps. I walk up the steps and sit on a wooden bench that stands to the right once I've got to the top. I'm looking at my shoes, brown, worn out leather boots. I take the striped scarf off my neck. I take off my leather jacket and tug the white, crumpled cotton T-shirt away from my chest and let the air inside this cold building play around my bosom. From the opening bursts a rhythmic sound; my heart beating its way out of my mouth.

A door opens to the right of me. A young woman in a dark-blue skirt suit, her hair neatly arranged, holding a piece of paper, addresses me by my surname, my father's name, and welcomes me. I follow her into a narrow passage. She extends a hand to me, offering to take my jacket and scarf as she nods her head toward the door at the end of the passage, which stands open halfway. In there, a chair appears. In the middle of the hallway. A chair I've waited to settle into as far back as I can remember.

I'm sitting and looking straight ahead at five people seated along a long table seeming not to pay any attention to my being here. Furthest left is a rather chubby middle-aged man, bald. Totally. He is dressed in a white, long-sleeved cotton tee. Next to him is another man, long-faced and birdlike, dainty even though his skin is coarse; slender, he has a crumpled cotton scarf around his neck and is wearing a light-brown shirt underneath a brown tweed jacket. The third man? An angular face, yet swollen. His gaze harsh, like a hawk, yet still in some strange way sluggish. He seems drunk. He is scruffy compared to his neighbor, man number four, a young man in a light-blue shirt and blazer, his curly hair combed back. Right eye involuntarily blinking. A gold ring on his little finger. At the end of the table, to the far right, sits a woman. Probably fifty-two years old. Or three. Light hair down to her shoulders, a long nose, gentle eyes. No or little makeup.

Blazer breaks the silence with a formal address, giving a short speech while he looks at the screen on the laptop on the desk in front of him. The others leaf through papers. Papers about me. Now they all look in my direction. Had I been asked questions while my attention was focused on people's appearances? My silence at the hypothetical questions proves strategic when Chubby poses a question about how to depict the sky. I had expected this question and answer confidently. I say we need to look back to the origin point. At aesthetic and emotional experiences, using the academic principles as a guiding light. We need to take up the thread in the belief that history could have turned out different than it had once impressionism took over from romanticism.

With these words of mine, the five all become one. They unite in a stirring silence that now clashes inside the hall. And lasts until the woman comes to my rescue by leading the discussion from the theoretical to the personal. She asks me why I am enchanted by landscape. The theme of the sky. I answer, in a shaky voice, that it is the fact that the subject lies always in front of our sight, real and material yet untouchable and unpredictable. She looks straight into my eyes and I think she knows I want to say something more, but am hesitant. I look down and then up. Chubby leans on the table, hiding his face in his hands, looking like he's sleeping. Bird looks right through me. The drunk Hawk is about to drop off. I look at Blazer slowly and calmly turn the gold ring on his finger while he lets himself peer into the computer screen. The woman is still looking at me and now she smiles. Then I look back down. I take my ring finger, run my fingertips over the stone Dad gave me and think of his words. "To be yourself?" Something of that sort because, written on my mother's forehead, who still tried to agree with Dad's words with a gentle smile, were the words: *How on earth can you be anything else?* But does it matter what I say? I think. Because when I speak, *I* speak. I can, of course, choose from a few versions of me, but the one that gets selected becomes *I* as soon as I speak. And so I start, without preface:

A little girl in a small-sized city is out walking with her mom, who holds her daughter's palm with one hand and uses the other to point out a mountain that rises high above the city, naming it. The girl knows the mountain's name but points up to the sky. To the light beyond the clouds; she asks what it's called, that opening. Mommy says she doesn't know, that the girl needs to find out when she grows up, find out and tell her. There is only one way. And so the child's destiny was set.

As soon as I set a period after my words, I realize that this little story I just told, which has been told on countless occasions, arousing the admiration of all its listeners, is nothing but sentimental nonsense. The story is meaningless; it does not apply here because it does not answer the question that has been proposed. Rather, it bears witness to the temperament and inattentiveness of the applicant summoned before this board to show herself worthy of admission to this temple of art. That's how I tear myself down, deliberately, to prepare for the worst. But when I look up, I see that my hypothesis has been confirmed: The gentleman at the computer knits his brows. Then he turns to Bird, who has not said a word since I walked into the hall, and asks if he would like to add anything. He shakes his head, distracted, but the one who was sitting between the two, the drunk one, has disappeared. He seems to have departed the hall when I was in the middle of the story about me and Mom and the clouds that stood out against the clear sky. Without my noticing.

I don't remember having left the building, only having stood under the bare ceiling on the top step, a six-meter high pillar on either side of the door behind me. A vacuum filled my head, a strange disquiet, I heard music from the floor-to-ceiling window to the right of the entrance. It was being played on a violin, but elsewhere I could hear a piano. Was someone trying to perfect the perfect music recital, or to interpret the tune in a way that must surely have been done before. Or was music being written? Trying to find the last combination of available musical notes, which are self-evidently in scant supply given how much time has elapsed since the beginning of composition. And the eternity that lies ahead. Are there fewer remaining possibilities in this field than the one where people strive to rearrange words, to stretch the shape of written language in all conceivable directions? Are there rules still extant in prose that have not yet been broken? Firmer boundaries, ones that creative types imagine are present even though they no longer are? I silently curse time. In the arts, time is nothing but a destructive force; the challenges of science, on the other hand, are unbreakable, causing our wrestling with them to be more constructive as time becomes the future. In science, you open doors for whomever comes next; in art, you slam doors shut behind you, causing the story to gradually wind down: it is now at an end. Not because the distinction between non-art and art has long since disappeared, but because anyone who wants to start up a story, to continue to spin the thread of visual experience, cannot progress forward because both subject matter and technique fix the imagination, restrict creativity. And our world cannot refresh itself fast enough to feed us new illustrations for old methods. Put another way: how many pictorial versions of people can we make? Is there something beyond the idea of distorting faces and bodies, expanding the gluttonous flesh out into the infinite, creating dismay and alienation with a mess and a mash that soon enough undermines its original craft? Such novelties are worn out as soon as repeated. Is there somewhere a picture of clouds that has not been painted? I had intended to convince the five at the long table that there is, but I no doubt failed.

Poor wretch that I am, not even the future will succeed in throwing the past's glittering resplendence on contemporary art, for everything has been used up, over and done with. Looking down the steps, trying to remember how many there were, an idea almost comes to me. Hazy at first but with repeated attempts to reach for it, each time not quite grasping it, I move ever faster down the steps, soon taking two at once, and as I approach the last steps I jump, airborne.

I'm in the air a long time and soon realize I've made the wrong choice; the landing is going to be painful. However, to my great surprise, I land with both feet on the ground. In front of me, a crowd mills busily by the building across the square. Something has changed, the city suddenly so grayish, all at once murky to my eyes. People's movements are also somehow cruder, abrupt. But I can't stop to think about that any more. I'm in a hurry. My path lies along a street off the square to the right of the building. There, in the corner, in front of an old textile store, two men stand with hands in rumpled overcoat pockets. The men talk without speaking any words from their lips, just nodding to each other, eyes fixed on the sidewalk. As I pass, one of them looks up, toward me. For one moment, I feel like it's Bird, from the interview, but by the time I am ready to look again and see if it is so, the men have gone.

Now I head back to the right, into a narrow street. Past old buildings that seem to collapse over me; as soon as I arrive at my destination, I go straight for shelter. Directly into a large and smoky kitchen. There I can see the outlines of two older women at work. I walk through the kitchen and open the door into the hallway. I walk along the elongated corridor, which opens at its end in two directions: to the right four steps lead down while in front of me there are steps up to the next floor. As I head upstairs, I see they turn to the left, and then my path goes left again, up three more steps. And yet again to the left, this time four steps. And then the same story: back to the left and up, and when it's over and I look right, I realize I'm looking along the same corridor from which I had originally entered. I go back along the hallway and decide to ask the figures in the kitchen how to get up to the next floor. But when I open the kitchen door, I realize I must have mixed everything up because there's no kitchen, just a big room, some sort of atelier. Up against the wall opposite the door there's an old writing desk, and at the desk sits a young woman, leafing through papers. She's wearing a black dress, short but flouncy, with light-colored stockings and high-heeled shoes with buckles. Around her neck is a lightweight scarf, but her covered hair is unbound. I probably should announce my presence to her, but hesitate for a moment when she raises both hands into the air and lets out a sound, a half-howl, which does not sound exactly like a cry, although her hand gestures indisputably signal this. Then she gets up and walks into the middle of the room. Up against the wall stands an easel; on it, a small painting. I follow the woman. The image is a brown area on a light background. An abstraction, some sort of Russian Suprematism from the early twentieth century, it seems to me. I move a little closer and see it rather might be a miniature landscape; the light background seems like a frame around the image. Growing altogether uncertain, I get closer, standing right behind the woman. Have I seen this before? I ask myself, looking at the canvas; a picture of the back cover

of a painting. Concept work, maybe not very original, I think as
I realize it's probably high time to account for myself. But just
before I address the woman, I take a few steps back for safety.
When she does not seem to answer my greetings, I walk back
toward her and place a hand on her shoulder. Still no response so
I walk in front of the easel and nod politely. She does not seem
to see me, but what I see strikes me as even more amazing than
the possibility that I'm invisible. As soon as I turn back, an awful
brightness creeps through the window behind me and illuminates
the artist's face, the swollen nose over the tired mouth. It's a man.
And not a man in women's clothes, rather a man from far away
in time. I get a final confirmation of that when I look away from
his foul-smelling face and out the stained window in the corner
of the room. By the riverbank, a lot is going on. There' a tied-up
sailboat; out on the river, men punt and row small dinghies. I
think about the painting on the easel. Could it be? I turn around,
planning to get a better look at it, but the artist is standing right
in front of me, and sticks his foot out as I walk past him. I fall
to the floor and crack my shoulder painfully against the stone,
but when I try to get to my feet, someone puts a hand on my
head: "Are you okay, love?" An elderly woman in a light poplin
coat with a thin nylon scarf about her neck thrusts her worried
face in front of mine and extends her hand to me as I lie there by
the bottom step. Some passersby have stopped and watch me as I
crawl to my feet and limp away from the big building. Dragging
my hurt leg out into the square with my right hand on my left
shoulder.

I can't say exactly what happened as I lay there, insensible, it
could hardly have been more than a few seconds, but I know the
thought I'd had at the top step had not left me on the path I had

chosen. My attempt had been to look at my existence as a past and try to revise it as a historical period, as I'd loosely outlined before the Five; an attempt destined to fail. I had meant to re-experience moments from the past, trying to break down their working parts and so discover each thread of the visual experience within them. I had ended up in a different place than I had meant to, but that didn't matter, the result was the same, the message simple and oft-repeated: intellect, not emotion, controls our visual perceptions, our experience of beauty. The result: that people can only be citizens of their own time. Or, as Mom always said, "How could anyone be ahead of his time?" I felt that was the one definite thing restricting human artistic creation amid the uncontrollable vacuum of expression, with the exception of history where statements no longer have meaning. The thought of a painting's distant future was almost too much for the imagination to bear.

Well, all of those weighty speculations proved pointless. The envelope from the Royal Art Academy; I opened it carefully in front of my parents, reading the letter and reporting the decision by shaking my head. Mom's face betrayed no emotion, but my Dad made a face that merely intensified my irritation over the situation I had ended up in; in his mind the rejection was nothing more than a conclusion based on the most talented professionals' judgment. Mom knew that perhaps things weren't so clear-cut, but she did not say anything because the idea of the misunderstood genius cannot be put into words except in jest, mockingly; a genius needs to be discovered to have been misunderstood. Until then, he's not misunderstood, and consequently he's not a genius. In addition, there's nothing she could have said in the present circumstances, she couldn't urge me to persist, because it was she who had indirectly given me the signal that the second-best school would not be enough if I was going to amount to something in this field. So it was strange, given this, that she did not seem particularly convinced of my talent, a conclusion I reached based on how she chose the scant few artworks of mine that she put up in her house.

I went up to my room, shut the door behind me, and lay down in bed. I looked at the ceiling above me and thought to myself that maybe Dad's understanding was the correct one, even if it was based on ignorance. But that realization did not help me much: preparing for this entry exam had taken me two years and now I was back at the starting line. I did not know what to do, but I knew that the story of the little girl and the cloud that stood out against the sky would not be the story in this house anymore. Then I heard voices outside my window. I got up and peered through the blinds. The industrious and virtuous upper class were taking hands to their own garden as a way to distract their minds from the bad news. Mom—perhaps already having the idea I should study art history at Hans's school—in her scruffy gardening outfit, shears in her gloved hands. Dad starting up the lawn mower. I carefully closed the slats.

The street soon reaches its end. From here, the way to my parents' house lies uphill to the right. I walk faster, slow down, then suddenly stop and take a few steps back. In the window of the antique shop two houses from the corner stands a girl. I bend down and put my face up to the glass. It's her! With a scarf on her head, a goose under one arm, leaning back a little as if to balance the bird's weight, so that he won't pull away from her grip. A porcelain statue my dad gave Mom before I was born, a statue with an emotional resonance I never understood. I just knew that those feelings must have run deep because such ornaments were never to Mom's taste and she was not one to value anything of which she did not approve. And that's why, too, I flung the statue against the floor in one of my teenage moods, after Mom had banned me from something she did not like. I watched her cry over the dead object, knowing despite my lack of insight that her tears related to the story behind the gift. However, I had no concept yet that maybe Mom was crying over the loss of a child, the barrier all parents of teenagers cross when their offspring become distant, alien beings. But now the goose girl is standing here, a telltale sign that what has once been broken can be mended again; my meeting with Mom will be perfected with this gift!

I decide to obey this turn in the narrative, pushing the door open to the sound of a bell. There's nobody inside, but after a few seconds a white-haired man appears in one corner of the store. As though he effectively jumped up from the floor. The attendant welcomes me, quite softly but with a polite gesture. I point to the statue in the window. He nods his head approvingly, reaches for the girl, and shows me the price on a crumpled label under the pillar on which she stands. It seems to me for a moment that it might be the same price my dad paid for this little object back then. The man puts the statue on the counter, reaches under the table, and gets a cardboard box, rather big for such a small object. He asks if the girl is a gift and then gently places it inside the box, but only, it seems, to take it back up and lay on the table. He shakes his head and disappears into the room behind the counter. The statue is a dust trap. The white-haired fellow is going to get a cloth.

I look down, wondering if the statue is such a clever idea. Whether I shouldn't ask this obliging antiques dealer for a smaller and perhaps more cushioned box than the one here on the counter, in which lies some scrunched-up old newspaper. But when I look down in the box I see a face inside. An obituary accompanied by the photo of an old woman I know, a woman who died at home and was being buried in Reykjavík cathedral on 10 December at 1:30 P.M. Madam Guðlaug Otterstedt. My grandmother's sister on my mother's side. I don't remember being at the funeral. Presumably Hans and I had already moved abroad. But I remember one of the few times I met this old woman. "Aunt" Otterstedt, a woman Mom and her relatives whispered about a lot when recalling the old days. It was my uncle's sixtieth birthday. At the time, this lady was probably well over ninety; she sat in a wheelchair over in a corner of the living room. I roved from one room to another, in my own world, like any teenager, waiting for the gathering to come to an end, but the old figure was all alone there in the corner and when I went to one end of the dining table to grab a bottle of soda, she tugged on the knot which I had, contrary to my mother's wishes, knotted in my thin cotton tee at my left hip. She asked me if I wasn't Mom's daughter, and when I assented, she pointed to the chair next to her, commanding me to sit. Taking my hand, she put her aged but silk-soft palm over the back of it and started to ask me about my schooling. When I told her I was rather indifferent to high school, she hammered on about how important it was I get through school. I must complete my exams. I told her I could manage that, but then she started talking stuff about women's education, a jumbled, rather incoherent speech, yet when I made a move to stand up she caught my hand. Suddenly, her speech became clearer, and she began to tell me a story I somehow managed to listen to with one ear; half my head back then was wrapped up in selfish thinking, I was never able to fully concentrate on anything not directly related to myself. But with that one ear, probably the left one, I heard a story that I did not forget as fast as other things that involved the world beyond my own. Perhaps it was Madam Otterstedt's narration I found memorable, perhaps the scenes in her story. But I never fully understood what or who the story was about, because when Otterstedt came to her narrative's end, as she clasped my hand tightly, seeming about to follow up her words with some explanation and more detailed information, I saw Mom in the next room giving me a firm, unambiguous signal it was time to leave. We were off; I half-sensed, there in the silence in the back seat of the car, that our sudden departure from the big birthday somehow concerned the friction between Mom and her sister Greta. I pressed my face up against the car window and disappeared into my own daydreaming about some clothes and two boys. I stopped thinking about the story, and did not remember it for many years. Little by little it dissolved, and at moments in my life I would have insisted I'd never heard it. But now, standing here at the counter, in front of a door that seems to lead to the antique shop owner's apartment, where he's gone to look for a cloth to clean a porcelain goose-girl I've decided to give my mother, Guðlaug Otterstedt's narrative rises before me; the sentences arranged one after another, and I realize they will finally get their meaning, once put together into a whole. In my retelling, it goes like this:

It's early in 1960. A high school history teacher is standing up at the chalkboard. An older man. He has his hands behind his back and is talking about art and an artist; I remember a little bit of how this story went because Otterstedt deepened her voice to imitate the teacher: "His art must be examined without prejudice, not in light of the fact that he had the destiny of the whole continent in his hands. On his shoulders! But yet we cannot separate the two things: because his ability to find the essence of any problem he never needed the foundational education one gets in art school." Then he looks down, "One could say he approached the canvas and the battlefield the same way."

Students write in their composition books. All but one. A girl. She sits motionless, leaning on her table that's placed by the window, holding both hands to her head. In one ear, she receives a story about Iceland's occupation, that "great fortune in misfortune," as the teacher puts it; at the same time, the girl is also thinking of a conversation she heard in her mother's kitchen a few days earlier, a discussion about old family matters. The powerful voice of the teacher resounds with double force inside the girl's head so she puts her hands over her ears and looks out the window. And there's something happening. The girl stands up to the glass: a gleaming, polished Humber Pullman (here I think Otterstedt may have embellished in light of later knowledge, it's certainly not my addition) is driving into the square, Kirkjutorg, in the very center of Reykjavík. The car parks right by the cathedral. Two jacket-clad men in Knox hats (here, again, all her) get out of the car. They open the backseat door. Out steps a third man. He's wearing a very dark-blue sailor jacket, cap on his head. The three men, along with an entourage from somewhere else, head toward Parliament. Crowds stream along Skólabrú, but what captures the attention of the high school student is what is happening at the edge of the scene. In a small attic room in the house on the corner of Skólabrú and Lækjargata, a young girl is standing at the window. She's wearing a floral dress with short sleeves. Her hair is parted in the middle and pinned back with two barrettes so that it fans out on both sides, her shiny locks flowing down to her shoulders. Behind the young girl stands a middle-aged man. He is wearing a uniform. The man moves closer to the girl. He takes her slender waist, buries his face in her little collarbone and pulls her away from the window. The girl takes hold of the curtains and draws them so that everything disappears. Everything except little hands grabbing tightly to the curtains like they might rip them off and then a man's massive face overlays the picture: the exercised history teacher mirrored in the window. The student can see herself with her hands over her ears, her own horrified expression in the glass, and behind her the teacher, stroking his head in confusion; then a wholly arrogant smile plays across his countenance: "Of course you must know, young lady, all about how the event I've been laboring over took place, all about its significance for the Icelandic nation, for her children at such a precarious moment in history? To know your nation's history and the men who shaped it is every man's . . ." but before the teacher can continue his speech, the girl gets out of her chair and rushes out the classroom and out the school building and down the steps, across the street and up to the building at Skólabrú. She stands at the front door, looks around and begins to beat on the door, unrelenting. She starts yelling for help. The teacher looks out the window at this, together with his students, some of whom have actually gone outside and stand there rigid, watching their classmate's behavior until one of the boys in the group goes after the girl who is now leaning on the door, holding her forehead, dead on her feet.

The following day, the girl gets called into the principal's office with her parents; she's made to explain what happened. At first, she has no memory of it; then, under interrogation, says she saw a soldier, or rather some sort of officer, about to assault a young girl up in an attic room in the building on the corner. She had actually already realized that the image she saw out of the window came from a former time, that it was hardly of this world, but she could give no other reason for her behavior as she sat there between her parents, next to her mother who put her hand over her mouth when the principal explained defiantly that the school authorities had knocked on the door to the house right after the tumult and found what they already knew: there were men working in the house, hanging wallpaper in the rooms and working on the floor up in the attic. The authorities were welcome to look in but not to step on the floor. The paint was still drying.

The girl was sent to a doctor, who said he believed her suffering stemmed from headache attacks; if he mentioned hallucinations, that was never discussed within the family. Indeed, the atmosphere in the wake of the event became more difficult every day as a result, and eventually led to this superior student divorcing herself from school and half-fleeing abroad with an older girlfriend. The family's explanation for the girl's decision was that she simply did not have the focus to complete her matriculation exams.

Voila! The silver-haired antiques dealer extends a coarse but clean hand invitingly away from himself in the direction of a golden box standing on the store counter. Then he puts a finishing touch on the work by pulling tight a black silk ribbon he has bound around the package. I smile and thank him. Have I paid for the statue? I ask myself as I stand on the upper steps in front of the store, the box under one arm. But I'm not able to answer the question. I can't even take a step down to the sidewalk due to a sudden, paralyzing realization as to my petty, narrow mindset, which the day's haphazard events have striven to reveal. What had that message from Bonný been, the one I read inside the passageway just now, except a sign that I have made my friends nothing but fictions of my own imagination? A message that I am constantly reading my own vulnerabilities into others' actions and behaviors? Sigga's call? Bjarnfríður Una's heroic act in the Near East and my cowardly behavior at the same event? What was the difference between Hans's indifferent response when I lay in the Icelandic National Hospital after my miscarriage and the handball coach's actions when Ester gave birth to their youngest son? Perhaps that Hans was situated only two kilometers away from where I was suffering, while Ester's baby was born two months before the due date and the sports tournament was not some divisional contest but a national game overseas? Who had talked to the young composer at the dinner party? Me, or Mom? And Aunt Otterstedt's story? I remember it as though it was yesterday that she told me about the winter of 1960. And what had happened? Had the girl studied abroad? In London? I would have known if I'd asked and listened and believed Grandpa's last words instead of letting myself be satisfied with Grandmother's words, who thought it was better to believe that her daughter left school because of learning difficulties than because of mental illness. Better that the girl was foolish than rebellious and perhaps disturbed; of course, it was nothing but a result of the damn migraines which I'd inherited and which Mom, for a variety of reasons, had never talked about. And after I grew up, I nourished my immature annoyance toward Mom, abetted by the ever-lasting consequences of Grandma's fiction. This involuntary opposition to Mom, accusations about her being highbrow and haughty, were nothing but my own insecurity. Arrogance is not always a personality trait; much more often, it's the experience of those who believe they find it in others.

I was no longer completely sure what my real business visiting Mom was. I'd planned to confirm her silent approval from last night, indicating it would be better for everyone, including old S. B., that I submit my thesis. Even though I'd done what I'd done. But what on earth had given me reason to think that my mother was going to cover up a criminal act? Some casual aside she'd made, a half-answer to one of my father-in-law's foolish questions last night at a party? Yes, I was a true champion of over-interpreting others' words and always to my own benefit. More likely my thesis would not only be killed off by the single page I had flipped past without reading. It would be killed off because nothing supported my hypothesis other than subtle hints and some blinkered reading, being fired up to notice all the things that might support my theory, looking assiduously past any factors that undermined it. Until the unavoidable blew up on day 221.

At the corner, I turn right, up the street toward the church. Misconceptions? At that moment, a small white jeep reverses acrobatically to parallel park along the sidewalk. A woman sits at the wheel. She cuts the engine, gets out, and swings a bag on a hefty gold chain up onto her shoulder. Then she makes a motion with her key before looking away from the car toward me. Her hair is coal black, her skin is dark brown; she looks well weathered, like she's been around the block more than a few times. I realize at once who she is. I met this woman last year with my sister-in-law. It was the Christmas holidays and she was blonde back then. Some book club I was soon driven quickly away from after having partaken in dinner. This is her! Without doubt. Díana D. *Fear is that little dark room where misconceptions are developed!* But what's she doing here? Come to punish me for not meeting my "booked" time to discuss *the Demolitionist* and *unnecessary baggage.* We look into each other's eyes for about five seconds, until I glance away and continue up the street. But I have not walked more than a few steps before I hear footsteps behind me, a clanging crash in high heels drawing little by little so close that I think she must be right next to me. Unconsciously, I shift my route across the street, imagining I can walk all alone up the other side. But the high heels cross the street, too. Without thinking about it, and with quite a ridiculous twist, I plot a course in the opposite direction, down toward the city center. And now I walk as fast as I can without running, the sounds of footsteps at my heels. Until I reach the main street. That's when I decide to start running, an attempt to get across before the fast-paced traffic starts up and in that way get rid of this unexpected pursuer. I'm across; before I know it, I'm running toward a ten-story concrete lump that stands at the harbor right by the old shipyard. I order myself to stop, to put an end to this nonsense; it's absurd, I tell myself, but just when I'm going to turn around, I feel something protruding underneath my coat. Something hard against my chest. I grope under my coat and grab the damn notebook from the breast pocket of my night-shirt. Had I forgotten something when I walked out the door to my home earlier on? I'd meant to tear the pages with the nonsense about the *Demolitionist* out of my notebook. As the damp wind slips up under my coat, I realize that I never actually got dressed; I'm still in my nightgown.

I put the book in my overcoat pocket, finding I've reached the building. The footsteps are still chasing me and there are not many people around, so I don't allow myself to look but instead head straight toward the fire escape on the building's west side. The ladder zigzags between platforms, so when I get up to the first one, I know I will definitely see her as I turn to climb the next steps. But no matter how fast I try to get up the stairs, my pursuer is always out of sight, so tightly is she on my heels. And that's how it goes until we've reached the top and I prepare myself to start running along the length of the roof, though I know well that the only escape route lies back down. But I don't go far because my first step jerks me back, I'm hauled back toward the stairs. I've snagged my coat on the handrail, and when I tear myself loose with full force, it rips in two from pocket to hem. My notebook flies from the pocket, and when I reach out to grab it, it fumbles across the rooftop and skitters through the air. The book seems headed out of sight, but falls back down as it nears the roof edge, landing directly on the brink. And there the book lies while I throw Mom's gift away, get on all fours and move, with shaking hand, out toward it. But I can't go any further. A slender woman's hand takes hold of my shoulder. Here to examine my "baggage," I think, looking straight down the ten stories, down to the sidewalk. Then up and straight forward. Out across the harbor and the sea:

Professor John W. Lucy. He had given the green light. Deep down, I suspected he'd not read the thesis very carefully, but his comments were somehow in order; he seemed chiefly worried about the length of the thesis. I held to my line about the workmanship, and soon all that was left was to go over the direct quotes from the manuscript. I was on the home straight. I put the manuscript on the table and thought how I was going to miss this old tome. I went back to the book and opened it to day 221. I scanned the page but did not find the sentence I was looking for. I flipped forward and back and found another entry with the same number. This was the right one. The other entry I had never transcribed or read. I had clearly overlooked it, flipped right past. I did not realize then what had transpired, but now I think I know when and why this happened:

My discovery of S. B.'s gender had awakened a great zeal within me, an intensity that I had never known before, and I had worked well the years following my findings in the entry of day 203. But I was still the person I have always been: constantly thinking of something else in my environment other than I should be, always looking at people's appearances, gestures and hand movements while their words dissolved before me. Teachers. Lecturers. Fellow students. And the same was true in reading this manuscript; it was all too easy to disturb my focus. Rarely could I avoid looking up and noticing something else taking place in the reading room. How unfortunate, then, that at the moment I turned from day 221 to the following day, which had the same number, I heard sounds from the next booth across the way. They came from a middle-aged woman who on a regular basis discharged various strange noises. Sometimes it sounded like a piercing howl ending in a kind of bark. I immediately realized this was something that the woman could not control, but I wondered all the same whether she was allowed to, given a deathly silence was supposed to prevail. It was really annoying but when I looked across the room I saw that there was nobody except me who seemed be disturbed by the noise. Everyone was immersed in their own documents.

Actually, not all of them, and that's why I did not continue reading right away, but instead watched two old men sitting side by side next to a big table in the hall. One of them held a bound manuscript that the other was trying to take from him; when the latter managed to get hold of the book, the first would not let go. They sat there and fought over something that was obviously very precious to both of them, until the custodian came on the scene and tried to intervene; their bickering ended when he took the book back to the service desk. The two men sat there very still, both looking straight ahead.

There was no way that the painter S. B.'s daily pottering could take my attention from these two men. I had to know the ending. There wasn't long to wait, because soon one of them got up and left the hall. The other sat a little longer and looked down his lap before he followed suit. For a moment, I was on the verge of running after them to see if there was a sequel to the show outside the hall, but I let it suffice to look right down at the bound books on the shelf in front of me and wonder what in the world had just happened. What manuscript they had fought over. Whether the conflict had its roots far back in history.

I do not remember how long I sat there staring straight ahead, but when I finally came to my senses I quickly looked at my manuscript. And then at my transcript. Day 221 was in the computer so I moved on and wrote down day 222: *This day, after I was redie, I did eate my breakfast* and so on. A very dull day indeed.

Approximately five years later I sat there with this new page in front of me: Day 221. The second of two. The page that had been lying on the table in front of me while I watched life happen in the reading room, wondering at the history of people's behavior and movements, at a middle-aged woman's noises, at a strange conflict between two older men. The page I flipped past without transcribing and without reading, the page which overturned in just a few sentences my entire hypothesis, back then still taking shape, a hypothesis I was about to spend the next five years developing further and putting down over the six hundred pages that were waiting to be written. And none of this I realized until I was fine-tuning the thesis, checking one single word in one single sentence.

I looked at day 221. The second. And it was then that every-thing started to move, the lines running together, the letters start-ing to roll down the pages, changing to numbers, to monetary amounts. Pounds. Tens of thousands of pounds. How many days had it been? Six years. No, eight years, in fact, adding the two spent preparing for my failed entrance exam at the art school. A precious time for a woman my age. I was at the starting blocks, unsure if I'd ever have the mental endurance to get going again. I felt a heavy bang inside the right side of my head, my hands clenched. And then I put my thumb on top of the manuscript page, creasing it along the spine with my nail, drawing it down from a small hole that had formed at the upper seam; I put my trembling palms next to the opening, pressed one of them firmly down to the side, and somehow, barely voluntarily, moved the other to the side so that the page came loose. I pulled my hand back and looked around. The young custodian was nowhere to be seen; the elder one was at the front desk talking to Professor Barrington. What was he doing here? Were they talking about me, each smirking to the other? I put my left hand back on the page and then drew my hand off the table, the paper sticking to my sweaty palm as it vanished under the table top, traveling down to my skirt where the journey continued along my thigh toward the hem and under it to where it found my right hand, which had reached itself under the waistband ready to slip the page under a second layer, into my nylon tights.

And so this old paper lay pressed up against my flesh from where it did not come loose the whole time I made the long walk past Barrington, who seemed not to recognize me on sight, shaking his head and vibrating with the attempt to hold in his laughter over something his interlocutor had been telling him.

But my journey had no plan waiting at its destination. The sky-high walls seemed to travel with me, stretching out and bending down and toward me; I felt the books pouring out their shelves and coming down on me by the thousands; my miserable life would end buried by books, a 365-year-old manuscript leaf inside my pantyhose. No panties.

Suddenly all this devastation stopped. Hell took over. A new guard had clearly started on the job, a young woman, rather irritable. But what happened was more than irritation: when I reached her, it was like she'd received an order from above, or some other indication that I was heading in her direction. She looked right into my eyes and extended her hand, indicating she wanted to check my handbag. And she took her time. Opened all the compartments in the bag, flipped through the books. She opened up my laptop. Then she looked forcefully ahead, at me, but not into my eyes like before, she looked at my chest, leaning to the side of the front desk to size me up. But just when I was about to sink to the floor, she finally put the computer in my bag, gave it back to me and thanked me. I must have run out of the building, out the courtyard and onto the street where I gathered my breath. Then I left, getting swiftly out of the ancient city toward the suburbs.

The manuscript page kept its place at first but as I walked further, it gradually moved down my body to place itself between my legs. It was both uncomfortable and somehow felt more criminal than the theft itself. I could not really stick my hand under the waistband and tug the page upwards as I walked along the main street, so I decided to duck into an alley behind a supermarket across the road. When I got there the pain in my head was almost unbearable; I felt like I had to throw up. I leaned against a dumpster standing there. I lifted the big lid. The nausea increased and then everything came up from inside me and flowed onto the rotten fruit and other food remnants. I had nothing to wipe myself with, no paper in my bag, but that wasn't why I dug my hand under inside my skirt, into my pantyhose, and grabbed the manuscript. I was just trying to make my body more comfortable, but before I knew I had pulled it out of my tights, held it over the English garbage, and let go, grasping a box of expired cod fillets in breadcrumbs, and stirring the trash until the page couldn't be seen. I let the container lid drop and I ran from the alley—but as I stood on the sidewalk on my way back across the street, I realized that maybe this was not such a good idea. I had not meant to hide the page but to make it vanish, and of course there was a much better means to achieve that. I turned back. I was eager to recover the paper and, after stripping most of the dirt from it using the wall of the alley, I dropped it down into my handbag and went straight home. My bag clutched to my breast like a thief-fearing old lady. But when I reached home, my neighbor seemed to have some issue with me, about some things, beer bottles and other waste, that had disappeared from his backyard. It took me some time to get rid of him, and I was worried Hans would come home before I got inside. Then, when I was finally standing there alone at the kitchen sink with a match, I thought of Professor Shandy, Lucy's colleague, who had originally "found" the diary. Wasn't it likely that he'd browsed a bit in the manuscript, could it possibly be that he remembered day 221? The second 221? What if his memory of the entry was refreshed when the story of my theory began to circulate, maybe with the thesis already published in book form? Undoubtedly, it would be possible to tell from the diary that a page had been ripped out. The thread would lead back to me. Would I go to prison? But I

wasn't trying to profit from the past like others who steal historical relics. How would my intention be defined in court? And who
was the victim? The truth? History? The English? Was my larceny
and sabotage a victimless crime?

I decided to think the matter over until morning. I gently
caressed the page with a damp kitchen towel, wafted it back and
forth for a moment, and placed it in a book lying on the table-
top: *Sex, Gender, and Subordination in Early Modern England.*
And, inside that book, the document was eventually exported to
Iceland, because the next day never brought any answers to my
questions.

The woman's bony hand has released its hold on my shoulder as
I lie on all fours on the roof's edge, notebook under my palm. It's
safe to turn around. But what's facing me I already knew deep
down. Yet my first reaction is to retreat, and so suddenly that I
lose my balance as I get up from my squat position; with a single
motion I fall backwards. Back over the roof's edge. It happens
with an awful alacrity, but it's like the mind cannot immediately
grasp the journey it's on. Not until I feel the muscles of my body
tense, feel my breath get short. I start to fumble with my hands
in the air, so vigorously that for a moment I'm sure I'm heading
up and not down, following my notebook that slips from my grip
as soon as I start my flight. But, of course, I'm only headed for
the ground, fast, losing my breath as I see the book take to the air
and head out toward sea. And luckily so, because at this speed I
don't think I'm going to survive; better that the whole notebook's
contents blow out into the blue yonder. But I cannot look down,
I just watch the sky over the city while I try to catch at the air. I
think about my sister-in-law's words about mindfulness and the

importance of the moment, about the art of being present with which my friends, except perhaps Bjarnfríður Una, had become so familiar. No, there's no way to bring it all together, everything runs ahead of me, the question of how it ends horribly inevitable. What does history tell us? It's my father-in-law asking. What history? World history? I don't know, I've never read it!

And then it happens: I stop mid-air, float a little ways back up, flutter back and forth. My thinking becomes clearer, my perception stronger than ever before, and when the sky above me tears a hole in itself and the glittering sunshine descends to the ground it's like someone has set their palm under my nape and I've found perfect safety, like a young child floating in the bathwater with his mother's smiling face above him. Of course, Mom had had no intention of covering up a crime, but she will take care of things. As she always does. She whispers in my ear: "Mom will fix things." I have no idea how she will do this, but her words bring me a strange sensation. A peace and quiet I've never felt before and nothing could have disturbed save for the small fuchsia pink dot in the distance, in flight with the north wind toward the city. My notebook has changed course! And then I am back on my crash course to the ground, knowing that it doesn't bode well.

For my mother

Is the woman screaming more from excitement or terror? Impossible to say, but once she falls silent, it's more comfortable for anyone who heard to imagine her hullabaloo resulted from some kind of agitation, otherwise the silence might have meant force being applied, something held against the woman's mouth. If so, something would have to be done. Or the silence might indicate that she had been murdered. And so it's too late to respond.

Did anyone hear the noise she made, that awful sound? It's not at all clear, because there aren't many folks out and about in the stormy rain of this Sunday afternoon, and below the attic where the noise came from, there's no sign of life. The lights are off. Yet in the basement apartment far below, someone fiddles with a rusted window clasp. The glass is single-paned, rimed with sea salt, but through the pane you can see an old hand trying to open the window. The hand emerges from behind thin gray curtains; on a dust-covered window ledge, underneath brown flakes of paint, stand two plastic dancer figurines. Beside an old skyr tub full of mold. Once the hand has managed to push the frame out, the wind probes in through the window and the trash that blows along the sidewalk, light as leaves, lands variously on the pane or slips in through the cracked window. A paper cup rolls along the street and past the window and, following this, in the sway of a sudden strong wind, a small notebook. The book skitters across the ground, light enough for the wind to push it forward, but too heavy to launch it. The book is a little wet, so when the gust dies down, it comes to a halt right in front of the open window. The wind calms for the night.

The morning brings with it visibility. In the dead calm, a young man comes walking along the street. He catches sight of the little book. He reaches for it and without opening it or turning it over, he places the book on the ledge inside the wide-open window. Nonetheless—it was definitely not on purpose—the book lies half on the windowsill itself. And lies there late into the day until another hand appears from under the curtain. A child's hand. She holds a rather sickly plant in an old yogurt pot; it pushes the book back until it seesaws on the sill before finally falling back down to the sidewalk. And there it lies through the night and is still there the next morning when the hand, the old one, reaches out for the window clasp and closes the window.

The book lies there all the way to the next weekend. Before noon on the Saturday, a young man—not the same one who first set the book on the ledge—stands on the opposite sidewalk from the house where the hands live. The young man crosses the street, pushing a stroller before him; following him at a short distance is a little boy on a tricycle. The man looks back at the boy as he crosses, but once they are both safely over he turns and walks past the basement window. He rolls the stroller right over the book, but when he has passed the house, he suddenly turns around. He realizes the little boy is no longer keeping up with him. When the man sees the boy stretching his hand out for the book—its pink color caught his attention—he shakes his head and gives him a signal to let "it" be. At this very moment, there's an awful scream, some screeching from the attic window of the house: "Gummi!" The man involuntarily glances up but since nothing more can be heard, he indicates to his son to come along. The boy rides toward his dad and together they head west along the street. The child with the book in his coat pocket.

When the father and son get home, the boy has forgotten his plunder. He also does not notice when the book falls to the floor the next day at daycare as one of the teachers fishes the child's mittens out of the coat pocket. He is momentarily surprised, but puts the book back where it was. And where it will remain until the boy's mother puts the garment in the washing machine. That's at the end of same week. By then the story of the tragic incident a few days ago at Reykjavík harbor has come to light. But when the mother opens the book in the laundry room and reads the owner's name, there's no way for her to know it's connected to that affair: the deceased's name has not yet been published. But on Monday, when the woman's name appears in a death notice, the young mother somehow realizes she is, or was, the owner of the book . . . the right thing to do would be to return it to her relatives. By then, the book has been thrown in the trash, but what makes the woman go out to the garbage and dig it up are the manifest connections between the obituary and the news story about the tragic incident: the owner of the book was the deceased, and the deceased had died from an accident which simply must be the incident at the building down by the harbor. This connection, the suspicion that the book might contain important information about the "matter," is essential, because recovering the item is not particularly pleasant; the young mother had not slipped the book in to the recycling bin, for the obvious reason that the leather binding and the gold thread did not belong there. Instead, she'd thrown it in a plastic bag full of food scraps and other trash.

When the mother goes to look up the family of the book's owner, she finds two Hanses with the same surname. Neither shares a phone number with the deceased. In fact, the deceased is not in the phone directory, though her parents are. The woman writes their address on a piece of paper and puts it with some other papers in a little pocket inside the back cover. But after she has placed the scrap inside and is about to close the book, she claps eyes on the ink sketch on the final page. A picture of a woman. Her hair frames her face and covers one eye. The image is cut off at the chest and arms, one of which the woman in the sketch extends so she can inspect what's in her palm. A tiny little girl. That brings a smile to the young mother's face, and before she knows it, she's reading the writing under the picture:

I suddenly lost my balance. I stretched my hand toward Mom, know-ing it would not prevent my head from colliding with the sharp edge of the table in front of me. But everything happened differently than I thought; when I landed I lay in a soft hollow. I got up and looked around me, and suddenly the ground took to the air so quickly that I got a flutter in my stomach. I stumbled when I looked down into the murky abyss below this surface, which I could not figure out. Not until I looked behind me and saw how I was being supported. I was standing in the palm of a giant's hand. In order not to fall off, to God knows where, I wrapped both hands around its thick finger. I turned around, cautiously, toward his face. An awesome brightness struck my eyes, but using my hands as a shade I saw that the giant was not troll-like at all; he was somewhat delicate in his magnificent size, with silvery hair down to his jaw, smiling at me as he caressed my head so carefully with the index finger of one hand, cupping one hand over the other, a small roof, so that I did not pitch out when he started moving. He walked straight ahead and then went up to a slope. In the distance, I looked at green hills and still further off a mountain peak bathed in clouds. And above me, the sun in the cloudless sky.

We walked for a long time and finally reached the top of the mountain. Then the giant stretched his hand out into the sky, up over the clouds and pointed into them. At first, I did not see any-thing but gradually a picture appeared inside the vaulted ceiling, as though the sky was a mountainside and the picture lay at the foot of the mountain. For one moment, I thought it resembled a small village, though I did not see any houses. This phantasmagoria was illuminated but not by electric lights. Indeed, the light was so intense that I had to look away, back into the giant's face. The light behind him had been extinguished so I could now see his face better than before. I saw who he was. And at the same time, I realized who were behind him, though I did not make out any of the faces in the crowd. The men, neither giants not Lilliputians, were standing on tiptoe looking searchingly up into the sky. But only for a glance. Because they seemed completely untouched by this phenomenon beyond the clouds that could neither be set down in words nor drawn because it was completely illogical in its arrangement. But when I looked back, it was gone. The giant carefully upturned his palm and set me on the cloud. Plucked a fragment from it and spread it over me.

I closed my eyes, exhausted but glad from my journey, and knew that I would not have wanted to exchange this for all the sensations and sense of tolerance, all the kindness known as motherly love, some-thing I feel I often lacked as a child and teenager. Because the journey *had brought me a vision of my surroundings. It brought me the peace that only a sense of the aesthetic can bring, giving me an everlasting vista of another world where I felt delight and joy. And in that world, I knew I would never be alone.*

The young mother looks quickly up from the book when she realizes her husband is standing behind her in the kitchen doorway. Although he does not ask anything, she responds guiltily, slipping the book under a bunch of newspapers and brochures that have accumulated on the table.

The next few days, the paper stack lies on the table and continues to grow. For a while, a big, heavy case of beer stands on top of it. The woman had set it there because there was no other place for it once she had put two full shopping bags on the kitchen table on the Friday. The box stayed there into the evening, or until the husband realized that the weekend ale hadn't made it into the refrigerator. By the time he stuffed the cans into the refrigerator, and took a lukewarm sip, the beer box had broken the spine of the small book at its open back; the wife had not taken the time to close it before shoving it under the newspapers a few days ago, because she did not want her husband to see she was nosing about in other people's books. Not that he had any opinion on this or any interest in looking at the book. Indeed, the man had not even noticed what his wife was up to as he stood there in the doorway, and so now, as he stands with a collapsed, empty cardboard box of beer—he had finished putting it in the fridge—he takes the pile of papers out to the garbage. To where the recycling can, only recently allocated to the house's inhabitants, doesn't quite fit next to the trash can without blocking the kitchen window belonging to the people in the basement apartment.

The book's discovery, and its obvious connection with the harbor incident, occupied the young mother's thoughts a fair bit following the evening she read the text under the sketched portrait, but boredom at her workplace, difficulties with her marriage, and the struggle of raising two young children in rented accommodation, all that meant the book gradually disappears from her mind. Until one evening about a month later. She has a date with her girlfriends at a restaurant at the harbor, and when she reaches the place and five immaculate, fur-collared figures begin waving at her from the other side of the window, the scene of the story's action is unavoidable. The notebook resurfaces in her mind. She stands stock still a moment, meaning to walk through the door into the restaurant, but stops and takes to her heels, headed away from the building. The fur collars look at each other; one of them is about to run after her, but the others deduce she must have forgotten something, even if her reaction in fact indicates something quite different.

After a few minutes, the woman is standing in her hallway. She's standing in front of her husband, yelling. Shortly afterwards, they're both out on the driveway by the recycling bin. They lie the barrel down and dump the contents on the ground, and are rooting in the pile that forms at their feet when the woman sets eyes on the book, staring wide open at the top of the heap; it had been lying there on the bottom ever since the man threw it, together with the magazines, into the empty bin a month back. And luckily the receptacle had not been emptied all that time because the people in the basement apartment had, in a fit of anger, pushed it away from their kitchen window and up beside the garage just before the scheduled trash collection, and it seemed that the refuse collectors had refused to walk down there to fetch it, perhaps not convinced it would be possible to recoup from the inhabitants the additional fee such a stroll would warrant.

Instead of placing the book on the kitchen table and returning to the wine bar at the harbor restaurant, the woman decides to return the book immediately. She will do it tonight. But by this time, the paper with the woman's parents' contact details has disappeared from the book. Probably, it fell out after being placed in the recycling bin where the newspaper with the death notice also probably is. To go and root in all this jetsam for such small pieces of paper, or to scroll through all the pages in a vague hunt for the announcement, seems unthinkable right now; they must find the information some another way. But it turns out that it isn't possible to search death notices online, only obituaries. And the young couple doesn't subscribe to the newspaper that publishes them. The young mother is forced to call her father and ask him for help, and though he helps out at once, asking nothing, he does end the call with his daughter by reprovingly using back at her the words she used at him about getting a subscription to this right-wing newspaper.

In the autumnal dusk, warm light pours from the beautifully-illuminated living room; the home resonates prosperity and history, awakening the sense of security of anyone who glances in, giving the sense that nothing bad has ever happened here. It's the combination of artworks hanging on the walls that suggest this; old masters and emerging young artists in a chaotic but attractive jumble. The one bears witness to the intellectual health of people open to the new, the other that they have both feet on an established foundation. The image is perfected thanks to a slight digression in the foreground, on the window ledge: a small, porcelain goose girl, produced in Spain during the time of General Franco for the good housewives of this world.

The father comes to the door. He's a slender, supple man with graying hair, with a gentle demeanor, though he looks exhausted. No doubt is. And it dawns on him when the messenger explains her errand and hands him the notebook, now closed again with its slender gold thread. The father pulls them gently. He opens the book and sees his daughter's name written prominently in her own handwriting. He cannot come up with any words but conveys his thanks via a weak yet polite gesture as he closes the door.

Through the large window, the father can be seen walking into the living room. He extends toward the mother, who is sitting on the sofa, what he has in his hand. The mother examines the bound notebook, placing it up to her sense organs, like she's trying to smell her only child's last words. She loosens the thread and opens the book at the start, gently, and peeks in:

Meeting with Diana D. 30th of May at 14.00

May 25
Have I put my soul into some amateur's hand? Someone who means to help me get rid of the past. Help me seize the moment. Some dabbler who claims our troubles disappear as soon as they turn into words on a page. Oh, I know all too well about moments and words on a page!

May 29th
OK. Find this guy. The Demolitionist, who lives in the place we hide our secret thoughts. Rips everything down and tears it all up. Write

down his words and my reaction to his words and reflect on the extent to which I believe them myself and can approve of them.

I can't find the guy. Could the man be a woman? The lady who at all times has the words, whether she's talking or not. Irritating me with her constant presence. The one who gets to make all the decisions. In all ways in all places. An agent of strength thanks to her cunning, money and other privileges. Her presence is affected and hollow. Learned, but without insight. Her insecurity hidden behind a quiet voice, measured speech, lapping up the words of whomever she respects. Restless from attention-seeking and feelings of inferiority, all hidden under a safe, stable surface. So busy looking for beauty in every possible nook that she can't perceive what lies beneath. Holding in her hand a gift from her little girl: the Bethlehem stable standing on a paper base covered with cotton puffs; setting it aside and lifting up her hands before she hugs the child. But on Christmas Eve, the fragile stable has disappeared. Gets found on the thirteenth day. In the trash under the sink. The lady who scowls but only for a moment, so no one notices except me, her little one, then smiles at the furry, wondrously soft pink slippers. On the instep, a bow; on the bow, gleaming gems. But what a shame! They're not the right size! So the shoes go back into the box with the seal still on the soles, shiny plastic film, so she can get the right size later. The right size from the shop where I, her child, took the bus with all the earnings from my summer job and a bill from Dad, in case. Shoe size on a little slip of paper in my sweater pocket. But "later" never comes to pass. The lady who stands behind me in the mirror and lets me see the indifference in her face while I adjust my top's padded shoulders, the wide belt around my waist, the sweatband on my forehead, anxious and excited about the coming evening's adventure. And when the fateful night is over, she has no comfort for her child, just some obscure wisdom I cannot process until many years later when the wound has long since healed. Her perceptions are sharp and unfailing, but her knowledge of beauty is not the sort that increases human generosity, because what should have opened up her world tamped it down, closed it off, carried her off into misanthropy, her refinement marked not by anything but a disapproval of other people's perception and taste. In her narrow world, the world that fostered me, there was no room for diversity, only a few stereotypes. Chiefly aesthetes and philistines, types I defined myself by. The lady who takes all the decisions, with terrible consequences for her only child.

The mother looks up from the book as her husband places a teacup on the table in front of her. Out of consideration for her, he immediately sees himself out of the room, but had he not done so, he would have seen something he had not seen before: the totally expressionless face of his wife, called into being by the conflict of warring emotions. She's dressed in a worn white T-shirt, without a bra. Gray hair down to her shoulders.

She sets down the book, looks straight ahead, steadies one hand against the couch and gently lifts herself up. She stands on both legs, in her furry slippers, pink and downy soft; on top of each instep is a little silk bow. On top of the bow, by the knot, a little glass stone. A gemstone. She stands motionless, goes nowhere. It's as though the plastic film still on the beige soles underneath these old, unused slippers has stuck fast to the hand-woven wool beneath her feet. But it's quite the opposite: when she finally manages to lift her feet off the floor she slips on the mat and tangles her foot in the cord that runs along the floor from the wall, causing a standing lamp behind her to fall and crash down on the table where her teacup is, right next to the notebook. The lampshade, a world-famous porcelain design, falls directly onto the cup, which tips over on the table; chamomile tea spills out, flowing across the table toward the notebook, which now lies automatically open at a new place, a place the weight of the beer crate set on it broke it open to, the last page, revealing its ink sketch of a woman with an outstretched hand. In her palm sits a miniature girl wrapping her arms firmly around the woman's index finger. The woman's hair traces her jawbone, falls across one cheek, casting into shade her lips and rounded nose, but the eye that looks into the little girl's face is sharply drawn. From the corner of the eye over to the temple. The girl's face is barely discernible, but she seems to be smiling. And once the tea has flooded over these dexterously-drawn lines, it trickles in the direction of the words below the drawing.

The husband comes running into the living room when he hears the crash and his wife's scream. He bends down and attempts to help her to her feet but she pulls herself up quickly and fishes the wet notebook out of the tea. She shakes the book, in vain, roughly, causing the papers stored in the ripped pocket inside the cover to fall out. It's too late to save this open spread given how much water the paper has drunk; her first reaction is to put the book on the table and wipe the pages with her flat palm. And, of course, that causes everything to wash away. The drawing takes on a different look and the writing, the story about a giant and a tiny girl—which played no small part in the fact that a young mother from another part of the town undertook to look for the notebook in the recycling bin earlier this evening—is barely readable anymore. And it's like the mother knows what she's just wiped away with this frenetic drying because she collapses down on the couch, leaning on her elbows and holding her face in her hands. The husband finishes cleaning the table, but when his wife takes her hands away from her face, he inquiringly holds out to her the things that fell from inside the notebook pocket: a white business card and a small paper sheet, bygone. The mother takes the white card, reads it, and rips it in two disapprovingly; when she unfolds the old piece of paper, she's obviously very alarmed. She realizes immediately where it comes from, even though she can hardly read a single word as she holds the page right in front of her. The husband stands by her, totally rigid, until she commands him get her a magnifying glass.

After about an hour with the glass on the manuscript, the mother has managed to read enough words to understand what happened. Enough words to realize this sheet needs destroying:

The day 221

This day, after I was readi, I did eate my breakfast . . . Messanger from My Lord came to fetch my father . . . troble raisng the regiments . . . with Civill Warres between King & Parliament growing hotter . . . I had some talk wt my father and we took horses and rede into the Fields. After we Came back to house I myself went to my Lords house to have my hair cut round. Toward night I was in ye Chamber . . . my dutie as an Engliswan to enter into the sevice of my country upon consideration of my age . . . active body . . . rider . . . disgraise myself. Soon I set of with twentieth . . . assembled . . . troop of horses and to meet with my Captain . . . in the use of arms . . . capable of acting in case there should be occasion to make use of us.

The mother looks up. She acts like she's unaffected by what she's read, shrugging her shoulders at her husband. He doesn't ask a thing; in all likelihood he probably would rather avoid some legal hearing about his dear daughter, either now or at any other time. This is something his wife will solve, he no doubt thinks; he says he's going to bed, and heads up.

The mother is alone downstairs. Pacing the floor. She has the old page in her hand, possibly wondering if it's better not to tear it in little pieces rather than burn it. But she does not. She opens the cupboard under the sink, reaches down into the trashcan, and puts the page down inside. Then she goes up to bed herself.

But of course, she cannot sleep. She knows she cannot live any amount of time with a hundreds-of-years old cultural artifact in the trash under her kitchen sink. However, the other option is not viable: return the page and cause her daughter to be named a thief and fraud; cancel the thesis's publication. She could of course go to the library herself and restore it to its rightful place, but if and when the book comes out, there's a good chance her child will be ridiculed far and wide in the scholarly world. She must find another way.

She gets up again. She dresses in a thin silk robe and walks barefoot down to the kitchen. She opens the sink cupboard, reaches into the bin, retrieves the manuscript page and places it on the kitchen table. Then she fetches her magnifying glass and puts it over the sheet, runs it down along the page and slowly moves it, little by little, back up again: *to enter into the service of my country on consideration of my age . . . active body . . . rider . . . disgraise myself.* Disgrace? What was the painter's shame? The mother cannot answer this, because she cannot read the words that come before. But no manuscript specialist would be able to, either: only two letters of one of the words are readable; the rest, two, perhaps three words, are nothing but a blot. And, in fact, there's a little blot within the word itself, between *disg* and *ise*. She puts the glass very slightly closer to the sheet and sees then that there is no indication that in the blot there's an *r* or *a*. And though the text is written at a period before standardized writing rules, the wrong spelling of *disgrace* supports the possibility that an altogether different word has been written; in the blot, anything is possible, and maybe there's only a single letter. *U*?

And now the mother claps a hand to her mouth and closes her eyes and stands still for quite some time. Then she walks into the living room and sits at an old desk that stands in a corner. She puts on her glasses and takes out a thick stack of paper: *S. B. Diary of 1642 / 1643.* She reads through the transcription, pores over each entry of the diary in search of a clue. She is looking to confirm her suspicions.

Three hours later she stands up again. Stands in front of the shelves, looking for books. Returns to the writing desk and re-starts the computer. She does all this with great assurance, like she doesn't need to pause to ponder things, like she knows exactly what she's doing.

She gets back up at dawn. Takes a crisp plastic sheet out of the desk drawer and puts the manuscript, the diary page containing the testimony about day 221, gently inside it. She cleans the evidence away from the table top, reaches for a large brown envelope lying on the dining table, and takes another stack of paper from there. She puts it on the empty desktop. It's a manuscript proof; judging from its thickness, it's about 600 pages. Topmost on the front page is scrawled a short caption in red pen, but in the middle, printed, are the words:

Every Lovely Grace of His Face
S. B. Britain's first professional
female artist

She flips through. Looks for a long time at the sentence that will be on the page between the flyleaf and the title page once the manuscript becomes a book. From there, she continues to the table of contents. The preface comes first. Preceding twelve sections. The mother takes a pen out of an old silver cup standing on the table. The red pen. But when it comes to touching it down at the bottom of the page, she notices a motion outside. In front of the balcony door. She looks, but there is no one there, so she continues where she left off. The number 13. Point, curve and then: *S. B. Female Soldier in the English Civil War?* It will just be a short chapter, although there is no lack of scholarly literature to frame this little paper sheet, this remarkable document that has endured a long, difficult journey. One that seems to have had no reason at all.

Sigrún Pálsdóttir completed a PhD in the History of Ideas at the University of Oxford in 2001, after which she was a research fellow at the University of Iceland, and is the editor of *Saga*, the principal peer-reviewed journal for Icelandic history. Her previous titles include the historical biography *Thora. A Bishop's Daughter* and *Uncertain Seas*, a story of a young couple and their three children who were killed when sailing from New York to Iceland aboard a ship torpedoed by a German submarine in 1944. Sigrún's work has been nominated for the Icelandic Literary Prize, Icelandic Women's Literature Prize, Hagþenkir Prize, and DV Cultural Prize. *Uncertain Seas* was chosen the best biography in 2013 by booksellers in Iceland.

Lytton Smith is a poet, professor, and translator from the Icelandic. His recent translations include works by Kristín Ómarsdóttir, Jón Gnarr, Ófeigur Sigurðsson, Bragi Ólafsson, and Guðbergur Bergsson. His poetry collection, *The All-Purpose Magical Tent*, was published by Nightboat. He currently teaches at SUNY Geneseo.

Inga Ābele (Latvia)
High Tide
Naja Marie Aidt (Denmark)
Rock, Paper, Scissors
Esther Allen et al. (ed.) (World)
*The Man Between: Michael Henry
Heim & a Life in Translation*
Bae Suah (South Korea)
A Greater Music
North Station
Zsófia Bán (Hungarian)
Night School
Svetislav Basara (Serbia)
The Cyclist Conspiracy
Guðbergur Bergsson (Iceland)
Tómas Jónsson, Bestseller
Jean-Marie Blas de Roblès (World)
Island of Point Nemo
Per Aage Brandt (Denmark)
If I Were a Suicide Bomber
Can Xue (China)
Frontier
Vertical Motion
Lúcio Cardoso (Brazil)
Chronicle of the Murdered House
Sergio Chejfec (Argentina)
The Dark
My Two Worlds
The Planets
Eduardo Chirinos (Peru)
The Smoke of Distant Fires
Marguerite Duras (France)
Abahn Sabana David
L'Amour
The Sailor from Gibraltar
Mathias Énard (France)
Street of Thieves
Zone
Macedonio Fernández (Argentina)
The Museum of Eterna's Novel
Rubem Fonseca (Brazil)
The Taker & Other Stories
Rodrigo Fresán (Argentina)
The Bottom of the Sky
The Invented Part
Juan Gelman (Argentina)
Dark Times Filled with Light
Oliverio Girondo (Argentina)
Decals

Georgi Gospodinov (Bulgaria)
The Physics of Sorrow
Arnon Grunberg (Netherlands)
Tirza
Hubert Haddad (France)
*Rochester Knockings:
A Novel of the Fox Sisters*
Gail Hareven (Israel)
Lies, First Person
Angel Igov (Bulgaria)
A Short Tale of Shame
Ilya Ilf & Evgeny Petrov (Russia)
The Golden Calf
Zachary Karabashliev (Bulgaria)
18% Gray
Ha Seong-nan (South Korea)
Flowers of Mold
Hristo Karastoyanov (Bulgaria)
The Same Night Awaits Us All
Jan Kjærstad (Norway)
The Conqueror
The Discoverer
Josefine Klougart (Denmark)
One of Us Is Sleeping
Carlos Labbé (Chile)
Loquela
Navidad & Matanza
Spiritual Choreographies
Jakov Lind (Austria)
Ergo
Landscape in Concrete
Andreas Maier (Germany)
Klausen
Lucio Mariani (Italy)
Traces of Time
Amanda Michalopoulou (Greece)
Why I Killed My Best Friend
Valerie Miles (World)
*A Thousand Forests in One Acorn:
An Anthology of Spanish-
Language Fiction*
Iben Mondrup (Denmark)
Justine
Quim Monzó (Catalonia)
Gasoline
Guadalajara
A Thousand Morons

OPEN LETTER

WWW.OPENLETTERBOOKS.ORG